THESE HEROIC, HAPPY DEAD

THESE
HEROIC,
HAPPY
DEAD

STORIES

LUKE MOGELSON

TIM
DUGGAN
BOOKS

NEW YORK

TIM DUGGAN BOOKS and colophon are trademarks of
Penguin Random House LLC.

Library of Congress Cataloging-in-Publication Data
Name: Mogelson, Luke.
Title: These heroic, happy dead / Luke Mogelson.
Description: New York : Tim Duggan Books, 2016.
Identifiers: LCCN 2015035867 I ISBN 9781101906811
Subjects: LCSH: Afghan War, 2001—Veterans—United States—Fiction.
Classification: LCC PS3613.O373 A6 2016 I DDC 813/.6—dc23
LC record available at
https://protect-us.mimecast.com/s/wXm8BqCKapO1fn

ISBN 978-1-101-90681-1
eBook ISBN 978-1-101-90682-8

Printed in the United States of America

Permissions appear on page 187.
Book design by Lauren Dong
Jacket design by Darren Haggar
Jacket photograph by Andreas Ackerup / Link Image / Gallery Stock

10 9 8 7 6 5 4 3 2 1

First Edition

. . . why talk of beauty what could be more beaut-
iful than these heroic happy dead
who rushed like lions to the roaring slaughter
they did not stop to think they died instead . . .

—e.e. cummings, "next to of course god america i"

Contents

THESE HEROIC, HAPPY DEAD

TO THE LAKE

LTHOUGH BILL HAD BEEN A FULL-BIRD COLONEL in the United States Army, there was only one commander in the family. Every time I called I could hear her evil whispers poisoning Bill's ear. "Again?" that woman, Caroline, would ask. Then the sliding door would whoosh open, slam shut—a retreat to the deck—and Bill would say, "Just take it easy" or "You get to a meeting today?" Bill out there in the snow, looking in at the females, hand raised in a situation-under-control-type gesture.

It was going on a month that Lilly had been staying with her parents, at their lake house in Vermont. She'd left after the window broke—after I punched the window. It had been a bad scene: ambulances and police, concerned neighbors milling in their robes. I let her go. I knew that Caroline—who I'm sure to this day is convinced that I laid hands on Lilly—would do her worst to turn her. But I had faith in the colonel. Bill was a peacetime soldier—his twenty had fallen smack-dab in the sweet spot between Vietnam and Desert Storm—and in his mind, somehow, that was a debt he'd never quite repay.

There was no cell service at the lake house; every time I called the landline, Bill picked up, said Lilly wasn't ready to talk. Finally, I told him I'd quit drinking and joined a support group with the VA.

"So you're not drunk right now?" Bill said.

"I'm tired. The group meets early."

Bill promised to relay the news. When I called the next day, he told me, "Lilly's delighted you're doing that for yourself."

"I'm doing it for her."

"Still."

"Still, you can tell her to come home now. It's safe."

"That's Lilly's decision, son."

I allowed myself a swallow from my favorite coffee mug. It was my favorite because it angled out to a wide base that made it difficult to knock over, because there was often vodka in it instead of coffee, and because the wide base meant that the more you drank, the harder it became to reach the bottom.

"Some colonel," I said.

A few days later, Bill said, "I think I'm gonna have to put an end to this."

"End to what?"

"These talks. You calling here every night." There was a pause, and then Bill added, "Your belligerence. Your obsession."

"Let me talk to Lilly."

"She's afraid of you, son."

"Because of the window incident?"

"The window incident? The window incident? What she says, the window incident was the least of it. Did you tell her she made you want to kill things? 'Someday, Lilly, you're gonna make me kill something.' You never said that?"

"There was a context."

Bill sighed. "Stick with those meetings."

I called again—every few minutes, then every minute—but he wouldn't answer. In the end, Bill was the same as Lilly, same as everyone. People who did not respect the covenant of human relationships. People who believed you could just hang up, walk out. When the Stolichnaya ran dry, I fetched my Bushmaster and a box of ammo, stowed them behind the bench seat of my truck, and headed north.

It was blizzarding. Not far over the Vermont line the big flakes rushed the beams like I was at warp speed and they were star tracers in a wormhole through the galaxies. At the top of a high pass I spotted a pair of hazards blinking on the shoulder. They belonged to one of those vehicles between a station wagon and a minivan. Two sets of expensive-looking skis were clamped into the racks; the dome light haloed a man and a woman. I watched them watch me stagger through the snow. The woman said something to the man, and the man, still watching me, said something back. At first I didn't understand. Then I glimpsed my reflection in the paint of that car—the neck tattoo and face scar, that problem with my eyes. I motioned for the man to roll down his window.

"You OK, buddy?" he said.

He wore a turtleneck sweater and snow pants, and the woman, she had on something zippered and moisture-wicking. The man had only rolled down the window an inch or two; all the doors were locked—I caught the woman checking. She squeezed her hands tight between her thighs.

"I'm OK," I said. "Are you OK?"

"Us?" said the man. "We're OK, yeah."

He seemed to think it was my turn to talk. Eventually, he told me, "We're just waiting on the plows."

"Where you headed?"

"Nowhere," said the woman.

The man laughed. "Road's too slick to get down, is what she means."

"Think so?"

"I wouldn't try it."

I regarded the far end of the pass, where the road that had brought us all up the mountain dropped down its back side. "Is that just you, though?"

The man frowned. "It's treacherous. Every year, some joker—"

"Nathan," the woman said.

The man turned to her, turned back to me.

"But hey," he said, "you be my guest."

ONCE, DURING AN ambush in Kunar, I saw a private stooping to pick spent casings out of the dirt and put them in his pocket—proof positive of the old maxim "You fight how you train." Muscle memory, however, has its limits, and some knowledge defies inculcation. For instance, another maxim: "Slow is smooth, smooth is fast." That is as true, when you are all keyed up, as it is unlikely to be remembered.

I was halfway to the valley floor when my truck went sailing like a ship without a keel. The last thing I recall is a wall of white ice that looked like molten crystal—that euphoric breath before the boom, when your asshole puckers and you wait.

I woke to a teenager Velcroing a device around my neck. He was concentrating with his entire face. His mouth was closed; a rim of tongue protruded like a middle lip.

"He's conscious!" screamed the boy.

I pushed him off and climbed out of the cab. Up on the road, silhouettes stood among a fleet of four-wheel-drive SUVs, tall radio antennas and colored lights atop their roofs. The teenager was sprawled in the snow. "Just take it easy," he said.

"I need a tow truck."

One of the silhouettes stepped forward. He wore a winter hat with the earflaps down, a heavy coat with a star-shaped badge. A deputy badge.

"Only place that truck's getting towed to is the wrecking yard," he said.

I looked. The front end was crumpled against the escarpment and the windshield sagged on the dash like a limp sheet of Saran Wrap.

"You're lucky someone happened by," said the deputy. He was taking stock—neck tattoo, face scar, eyes—and not feeling reassured.

"Who?" I said.

"Called it in? Couple on a ski trip." The deputy squinted at me, like I was small or far away. "Said they saw you on the pass."

The teenager was proffering the neck brace—real cautious, at a creep, like he was fixing to snare a rabid dog.

"Is that really necessary, Mitch?" asked the deputy.

The question seemed to wound the boy. "Depends," he said. "If you mean is it mandated by the parameters and protocols of the National Registry of Emergency Medical Technicians, then yes—yes, Dep, it's really necessary."

"Just give us a minute, huh?"

After Mitch had sort of oozed away, the deputy explained, "First responders."

"Sure," I said.

"You mind?" Without waiting for an answer, he unholstered a Maglite and aimed it in my truck. "Gotta ask," he said, craning to see, working the beam. "What were you doing out here, conditions so bad?"

"I'm going to Lake Champlain."

"Got people up there?"

"Yes."

What they say about the way a man stabs versus the way

a woman stabs—how he holds the knife high, like a spyglass, whereas she holds it low, like a spatula? Same goes for flashlights, I would argue. There are aberrations, of course, and the deputy was one. He held his like a woman.

"Dep?" came a plaintive voice from the road—Mitch. "Can I at least assess the patient? At least got to assess, that's bare minimum."

I trudged over to the SUVs and sat on a tailgate. Mitch produced a stethoscope and requested that I lift my shirt.

"Damn," another responder, a Mitch-like slob with a chin beard, commented.

Except for the one on my neck, it was all heavy, martial imagery. Intense, I'd been told.

Also: gross.

Mitch was pressing the cold diaphragm against my back—reading the names, probably, on the tombstones there—when the deputy let out a whistle. He'd opened the door of my truck and was halfway in the cab, foot in the air. When he emerged he had the AR in his hand.

"Hello," Chin Beard said.

"That a Bushmaster?" asked Mitch.

"You betcha." The deputy raised it to a firing position, nestling the butt stock in his shoulder. "Seen one like it at the Brattleboro show."

"Brent has one," Chin Beard said.

"Like hell he does," said Mitch.

"He has one, Mitch."

"*Brent?*"

"Fellas," the deputy said.

He brought the weapon to one of the SUVs and laid it across the seat like it was a napping babe. "Relax, son," he told me. "You're in Vermont."

Later, though, after Mitch had completed his assessment and I'd signed a paper refusing medical assistance and we were all preparing to continue down the mountain, the deputy, as if he'd just remembered and was embarrassed to have to bring it up, said, "Oh, yeah. One thing. Those folks who called it in—the skiers? They mentioned that when they saw you on the pass . . . well, they seemed to think you might've had a few. Anything to that?"

THERE WAS ZERO legroom in the back of the SUV, and with my hands cuffed behind my back it was most comfortable to sit sideways, leaning on the door. As we headed toward town, the deputy would not shut up. He hadn't wanted to arrest me, he'd explained after administering the Breathalyzer, and now it was like he was trying to make amends. At one point, maneuvering a tight bend, he said, "Year ago, gal got decapitated here. Rolled her Benz with the sunroof open. Moonroof?"

The deputy waited for me to register an opinion. "I was the one found the head," he said. He glanced up to observe my reaction in the rearview mirror. "Guess you've seen worse. Me? That was a first. Head sittin' there in the bush."

After a while, the deputy looked in the mirror again. "I had to carry it back to the ambulance," he said. "That poor lady's head."

The sheriff was waiting at the station: Stetson, potbelly, mustache, and all. He eyed us and sniffed. The deputy guided me by the elbow down a bright white hall into a bright white room with a stainless-steel bench bolted to the floor and a narrow rectangular window in the door. I sat on the bench. Presently, the face of the sheriff appeared in the window.

For a long time he just stood there, the sheriff, gnashing on

a toothpick. Then he shook his head and left. The deputy returned.

"Bad news, afraid."

They'd pulled my record, found my priors. Because it was
my third DUI, there was a possibility of jail time. The rifle further complicated matters. Still, all might have been resolved—
patriotically, so to speak—had the sheriff, according to the
deputy, not recently caught his wife "in the act" with a national
guardsman. I probably noticed, when we pulled in, the absence
of any yellow ribbons on their patrol cars? "It's not that we don't
support the troops," the deputy assured me. "We support them
one hundred percent."

"So what happens now?"

"Now I bring you to County."

The county jail and courthouse was three towns over, and
in the weather it took us more than an hour to get there. The
deputy talked the whole way—mostly about Donna, the sheriff's wife. Seemed our guardsman was only the latest in a long
and prolific cuckolding career. Half the department had taken
a turn. Half the town. On and on the deputy went, maligning
Donna. It was obvious he loved her.

At the jail, the deputy brought me into a waiting room with
a plant and signed some paperwork that arrived via a drive-
through-style window in the wall. He spoke to whoever was
on the other side of that window in low, throaty tones. A door
buzzed and a guard appeared carrying a clipboard. He was
skinny, the guard, that was the main thing about him. The tight-
est hole on his belt hadn't been tight enough: he'd had to punch
his own. Since that fix he'd gone on diminishing. He stood with
his feet awkwardly far apart to prevent the sundry implements
attached to the belt from pulling it down.

"Ray," said the deputy.

"Dep," said Ray.

Ray was quadruple-taking—looking back and forth from me to the clipboard, clipboard to me. There seemed to be a discrepancy there he didn't quite approve of.

"He's harmless," the deputy said.

"Always are," Ray said. "Just like to think different."

MY COURT APPEARANCE was scheduled for the following week. The sole collateral I would have had for the bondsman was the title to my now totaled truck. The cell Ray put me into was four walls and a floor occupied by that caliber of men who were too broke and friendless to come up with the ten percent of their bail that the bondsman charged for posting the rest. In one corner was a toilet; in the other, a pay phone.

I dialed the lake house.

It was well past midnight and the phone rang half a dozen times before Caroline answered in sleepy bewilderment.

"Hello? Who is this?"

I was about to explain when a prerecorded message clicked on and a woman's impassive voice asked Caroline if she wished to accept a collect call from an inmate at the Brook County Correctional Facility.

"Oh, for Christ's sake," Caroline said, and hung up.

The next time I tried, Bill answered.

"Son," he said before I could get a word in, "I don't know why you're locked up, and I don't care. Just listen. If you're in Brook County because somewhere in that fucked-up head of yours it seemed like a good idea to come up here? To see Lilly? Think again."

"Bill," I said. "Colonel?"

But the line was dead. I brought the receiver down in a violent motion, stopped at the last second, and gave it gently to the cradle. I closed my eyes. When I opened them, a man in a wheelchair was grinning at me.

He had a kind of samurai ponytail done up in a bun, a down ski parka, fingerless leather cycling gloves, and bleach-stained sweatpants folded underneath two amputated stumps. Despite the missing legs, or because of them, his posture communicated a compressed ferocity. His posture was like a cranked-up jack-in-the-box ready to pop.

"What?" I said.

The man held up his hands, showing me the worn palms of the cycling gloves. "I was just asking myself, that's all."

I stared at him, waiting.

He pointed at my neck. "Who's Lilly?"

I'd gotten the tattoo a few weeks after we met. In retrospect, I suppose it was a bit much, a bit soon. I'd thought Lilly would find it romantic, be flattered, or something. My problem, Bill once told me, was that I had difficulty moderating my affection, which sometimes manifested in counterproductive ways.

I crossed to the far side of the cell and sat on the floor. The amputee followed in his chair. "Want some advice?" he said.

I looked away.

"Watch out for this bondsman. Me and Ruth been stuck with him for years. Tonight she'll have to put the mortgage up, watch."

Nearby, a man who'd somehow made it to the jail coatless, wearing nothing but Bermuda shorts and a black tank top, said, "How *is* Ruth?"

"Ruth?" said the amputee. "Ruth's Ruth."

The coatless man nodded. He pulled his knees to his chest and rubbed his legs. "I don't know how I got here. Do you?"

"I threw a hammer," the amputee said.

"At what?" asked the coatless man.

"Ruth," the amputee said.

We all watched an elderly fellow stand up from the toilet and lurch across the room. When he reached the pay phone, he grabbed the receiver and, without dialing a number, said, "Nurse? There's blood in my stool. Hello?"

The coatless man clutched his hair. "Throwing hammers," he said.

"Weren't no ax handy," said the amputee.

HIS NAME WAS Lee Boyle. He'd been infantry, a sergeant first class, and he'd been around. When, by and by, we got to talking about the wars, you could feel all the other stories crowding the one Lee wanted to tell—all the lurid impressions through which Lee had to reach in order to grasp the memory he needed. After he tried to tell me about his legs—it had happened after he'd finished active duty, moved to Vermont with Ruth, joined the national guard, and volunteered for one last, low-risk hurrah—I tried to tell him about my face.

While I was trying to tell him, Lee said, "Hold on. You mean that debacle at the mosque?"

"Debacle," I said. "That's nice."

"You were there?"

"Sort of. I was outside. I wasn't inside."

"Lucky you."

"Lucky me."

"So what happened to the guys who were inside?"

"Some copped. Some were court-martialed."

"But is it right? What they say they did?"

I shrugged. "I was outside."

After a while, the door opened and Ray appeared. He stood there like a gunslinger poised to draw.

It was Lee.

I WAS ASLEEP, slumped against the wall, when the sound of my name, pronounced as a question, began to penetrate the dream. *McPherson? McPherson?* Ray was reading from his clipboard. "Follow me," he said. "Or stay here, I don't give a shit."

We went down the hall to a wide-open room partitioned into cubicles. In one of the cubicles a hefty, frizzy-haired secretary was watching her computer and eating from a bag. Not far from her desk I spotted the drive-through-style window—the side of it from which paperwork was passed rather than received. The secretary brought over some files and the Ziploc with my wallet, phone, and cigarettes. "Sign and date here and here," she said, leaving two Cheeto-orange smudges on the page.

"What about my rifle?" I asked.

"Your what, now?" said Ray.

"That's evidence, baby," the secretary cooed.

Ray pinched his nose. " 'Baby,' Donna?" he said.

A revolving door delivered me into the night. A blueness was creeping into the black. The heaping white powder beneath which the parking lot was buried looked as fake and inviting as grassy hills seen from very, very far away.

Under one of the lamps sat a brown, windowless van. Thick gray clouds hacked out of the pipe. I could hear people arguing in there, a man and a woman. The van reversed out of its space and stopped in front of me. At the wheel was an unhappy, good-looking girl in a hunting jacket. Lee Boyle sat in the passenger seat.

"Get in," he said.

THE BACK OF the van had been stripped down to a bare metal hull. In the center sat Lee's chair. The foam cushions were warm, molded to Lee's shape. I had to wiggle around, press hard, to make them accommodate my own. It felt a little funny, like sticking your hand in another guy's mitt right after he'd played a game. No one spoke as we headed out of town; it was clear enough, though, how Ruth felt about Lee having paid my bail. She gripped the wheel like she was wringing it dry. At one point, Lee grumbled, "They're my checks," and Ruth said, "Your checks? Your checks? That's . . ." She shook her head.

We turned onto an unplowed lane that dropped into the tamarack and pine. A frozen stream paralleled the way, boulder tops and branches jutting through the ice. Now and then, we'd pass a yard full of tarp-covered crap, crap left out to rot or rust.

Lee and Ruth's place was deep in the woods, a single-story rambler with vinyl siding and a Gadsden flag hanging from the gutter. Ruth parked in the garage, beside a dirt bike with dry mud sprayed across its fender. I held the chair steady while Lee eased himself out of the van. (I had this notion you weren't supposed to help them much.) Ruth handed Lee a jumble of keys, and Lee unlocked the door. That was a thing of theirs, I gathered, him being the one to unlock the door.

"Plug it in!" Lee hollered as he wheeled inside.

Ruth groaned. "Jesus, Lee, can't we skip it?"

"We have a guest. Plug it in."

I heard Ruth rummaging around, bumping into stuff and cursing. Then, all of a sudden, the room came alive with frenetic blinking colors.

"Ain't it something?" said Lee.

It was something. There was more light than tree, every limb wrapped and rewrapped, alternating to a different pace and pattern.

"Had enough?" Ruth asked.

She was by the wall, hand on a switch. When she flipped it on, the ambient light of the ceiling lamp diluted the spectacle. Right where Ruth stood I spotted a small gash in the Sheetrock—and, on the floor, among bits of drywall embedded in the carpet hairs, a long-handled framing hammer. Noticing me notice the hammer, Ruth scooped it up and brought it to a cluttered bookcase without any books.

"Of course, he insisted on the biggest one," she said, waving at the Christmas tree. It was the first time Ruth had addressed me, but she did it with odd familiarity, as if I knew already that insisting on the biggest one was classic Lee. "I said not in a million years is it gonna fit. And voilà! It don't fit."

Ruth was right. The tree, by generous measure, was taller than the house, its top six inches bent at a right angle along the ceiling tile.

"Voilà my ass," cried Lee. "Look at that trunk. Go on, take a look at it. If they'd cut the trunk proper, where they're supposed to, it would've fit perfect. They left too much on, is the only issue with the tree."

They both turned to me, and I squatted low, to get a better view.

"Lot of trunk there," I said.

"That's what I been trying to tell her," said Lee.

MOSTLY, WHAT THE bookcase held instead of books were photographs of Lee with legs. An active, outdoorsy Lee. Lee overseas, Lee in nature, Lee on the dirt bike. Legs in every one. Legs, and also, in a lot of them, Ruth. A lusty, vigorous Ruth. A Ruth in possession of some feral tomboyish power transmitting through the eyes. One picture—taken at a lake, from up high, as if the photographer had been standing on an elevated dock—showed Ruth in shorts and a bikini top straddling a Jet Ski. Lee sat behind her, clinging to her waist. They were both laughing. They were laughing because that was a time in their lives during which the reversal of conventional Jet Ski positions could be funny.

I considered the Ruth on the sofa. She'd shed her hunting jacket and was wearing a plain white T-shirt. A bruise on her bicep bloomed like a ceiling stain. Sure, her husband had thrown a framing hammer at her arm; she'd just given a bondsman a lien against her house; and a stranger with a face scar was standing in her living room. She had every right to look fatigued. But still. Glancing from the bookcase to the sofa, sofa to bookcase, I felt like Ray trying to reconcile the genuine article with the info on his clipboard.

Lee returned from the kitchen with three cans of beer in his lap. He lobbed me one on his way to the couch, handed off another to Ruth. In exchange, she relinquished the remotes. I saw now that their TV sat on top of a different TV—the bottom one just had a mohair throw draped over it. Lee turned them both on. The top TV had picture but no sound; the sound came from the bottom TV, along with a bright salt-and-pepper square glowing in the mohair. His beer wedged between his stumps, Lee worked the remotes, one in each hand, jabbing as he clicked.

A pack of menthols lay on the coffee table. It had a glass surface, the table, and underneath the glass a bed of sand with buffed pebbles and seashells. Ruth gave the pack a shake, listening to hear if it was empty, which it was. I offered one of mine. When I held the lighter to its tip, the heat of that small flame seemed to thaw Ruth out a little.

"So," she said, "who's Lilly?"

Lee made a noise.

"What?" said Ruth. "It's a secret? If it's such a secret, why'd he get her name tattooed on his goddamn neck?"

"She's my fiancée," I said.

"Engaged?" Lee said.

"Basically. Almost. I'm gonna propose when I get up there."

"Up where?"

"Lake Champlain. Her parents got a place on the water. She's been staying with them for a while."

Something about this sounded off. "Her mother's trying to convince her to leave me," I explained.

Lee returned his attention to the TVs; Ruth put her feet on the table. "Kinda sounds like she already has," she said.

"Anyway," said Lee, "we'll bring you to the bus station in the morning."

RUTH LEFT THE DEN and returned with a stack of bedding. "The couch folds out," she said. "Lee, did you use that extra toothbrush I got you?"

When Lee, too absorbed in whatever we were watching to hear, showed no response, Ruth shouted, "Lee! The extra toothbrush I bought you! Did you use it?"

"To clean the .22 with," Lee said.

Ruth closed her eyes and appeared to perform a breathing

exercise. When she opened her eyes, she told me, "I guess you'll have to use your finger."

As soon as she was gone, Lee switched off the TVs. I was surprised. I'd thought he'd really been interested.

"Get your coat," he said.

A wooden walkway, raised on stilts above the snow, led around the house to a shed near the propane tank. Lee brought out from his parka the cord with the keys. He wheeled alongside the shed, undid a heavy padlock, and opened her up.

"There's a lantern," he told me.

I found it and turned it on. A rack mounted to the shed's rear wall held at least a dozen rifles. There were a couple shotguns, the .22 Lee had mentioned, and some badder stuff, including a tricked-out Bushmaster not unlike my own. All manner of hardware crowded the side walls. Most of it was for metalworking: lathe, torches, grinders, and the like. The contraption that occupied the center of the shed appeared to be the product of these tools.

I held up the lantern by its pail handle.

It was a sled, of sorts. A square metal frame rigged to four cross-country skis. After I'd dragged it out I found that the wheels of Lee's chair each fit snugly into a halved length of piping bolted to the steel. A set of bicycle handlebars had a bell attached to them; once he was situated, Lee gave it a ring.

"The skis were Ruth's," he said. "She used to be a big wintersports person."

"What's the plan?" I said.

Lee gazed up at the early glow kindling above. It was almost dawn. "There's some rope in there," he said. "We'll need that. Also, get us each a gun."

———

THE SNOW AROUND the house had been compacted enough to where I could take a few good strides, hop on the back of Lee's sled, and coast with him for a stretch, like you do a shopping cart. I had the Bushmaster slung on my back, and Lee had a pump-action shotgun in one hand. We were a couple of bandits on a cash-laden stagecoach—although, in truth, we didn't really need the guns. Lee'd said game sometimes hung around where we were going and it'd be a pity to find ourselves unarmed if a brood of grouse or a deer or fox showed up. I hoped they would.

At a tree with a strip of pink tape tied on its lowest branch, we turned into the woods. The snow here was untraveled, and almost right away the skis slammed to a halt.

"Rope!" barked Lee.

By lashing one end around the frame, holding the other over my shoulder, and really leaning in, I could pull him forward. Soon, though, I had to stop and rest.

Lee rang the bell. "Giddyup!"

"You son of a bitch," I wheezed.

It was maybe twenty minutes later—I was drenched in sweat, charging blindly—that Lee cried, "OK! Get some momentum and don't stop!"

I looked up and saw the clearing through the trees, a vast backdrop of light behind all those trunks and boughs. We were at the top of a rise that sloped down to it. I made for the drop. When the line went slack, I stepped aside, gathered it up, and tossed it on Lee's lap as he went flying past.

THE CLEARING TURNED out to be a lake. It was sizable, with a meandering shoreline that receded into bays and inlets, a wooden dock extending from the shore, small mounds of snow heaped around the pilings. Lee had glided out a ways, into the open, free of the trees that crowded the banks. When I reached him, he was tilting his face toward a warmth coming from the sky. There were colors up there now, wild ones.

"This lake is how come we moved out here," Lee said.

"It's pretty," I said. "No Champlain, but pretty."

Lee nodded. "It's how come we moved out here."

THE LIGHTS WERE ON, tree off. The den was warm and smelled of bacon. Ruth was in the kitchen, working a skillet. She had a cigarette in her other hand and was leaning back from the grease. She looked up, saw that Lee wasn't with me. I unslung the Bushmaster.

"He wanted to be alone," I said.

Ruth said nothing. I sat down at a square Formica table next to the refrigerator. As Ruth cut and stirred and whipped and flipped, the light grew in the kitchen, through a window above the sink. Suddenly, it was day.

Ruth placed in front of me a steaming mug and a plate.

"There's plenty," she said.

Hungry as I was, I had to take a moment to admire what she'd done. What she'd done was cut shapes out of the toast—circles, stars, crescent moons—and then fried eggs inside of the holes. I didn't know what to say. I said, "Lilly makes good eggs too."

"Lilly," Ruth said.

When I finished, she brought my plate to the sink. She squirted some soap. She was standing there, looking out the window, her hands in the suds and the faucet running, and she said, "I knew what he was building out there."

After a while, I got up and went to the sink and stood next to Ruth. She was still staring out the window. I followed her gaze to see what it was. There in the snow was the path we'd made with the sled. You could see it leading from the house all the way to the tree with the strip of pink tape hanging from its lowest branch. Then it disappeared.

"He thought I wouldn't notice they were missing?" Ruth said. "God I used to love to ski."

Just then a distant gunshot sent a few birds swooping out of the canopy. Ruth's reaction was so slight—barely a shudder—I wasn't sure she'd heard.

"Sounds like he got something," I said.

Ruth didn't answer. She was looking at that path in the woods.

SEA BASS

M Y FATHER, WHEN HE CAME TO SAY GOODBYE, could not keep his eyes off the Jeep in the garage. Hank Rubin had recently removed the top: its open cab, white upholstery, and padded roll bars seemed to promise happy times. The bougainvillea was in bloom. A bit dramatically, as if caching in the lungs one last whiff of the life that used to be his (even though, before Hank moved in and revived the garden, that bougainvillea had always been a scraggly, scentless vine), my father inhaled deeply through his nose.

"Well, then," he said. "I guess I better take a leak before I hit the road."

It was a six-hour drive to the place where he was going—a town I'd never heard of, outside Sacramento. One of his old army buddies owned a hardware store up there. "Orchard country," my father called it.

"Mom doesn't want you in the house," I said.

"I have to take a leak," my father said.

"What about the Shell?" I said. "You'll stop there anyway, won't you?"

My father grimaced. He contemplated the house, the Jeep, the bougainvillea. "Got a full tank," he said. "Besides, Kyle, that's hardly the point."

He marched to the flowerbox beneath the kitchen window, then, the one Hank Rubin had installed and planted with perennials. The blinds were up; my father, from inside, would've been framed from head to mid-thigh.

"Dad?" I said.

"Be with you in a minute."

After he'd shaken himself, he went to the wooden gate that accessed the back, pulled the string that raised its latch, and disappeared.

I stood there watching the gate. At some point, the front door opened and my mother stepped out. Noting my father's truck still parked on the street—the bed loaded with boxes tied down under a paint-spattered drop cloth—she said, "Where is he?"

"In the back."

My mother twitched. "Hank!"

Before Hank could respond, my father was crossing the lawn at a run. I didn't understand it until I saw the dog. When he reached his truck, my father yanked open the passenger door and slapped the seat. Lucy, our retriever, was there in a flash. My father slammed the door behind her and hustled to the other side. He turned the key and pumped the pedal. "Come on, come *on*," we could see him muttering.

Eventually, Hank Rubin joined my mother on the landing.

"What now?" he said.

My mother sighed. "He's stealing the dog," she said. "Trying to, at least."

We had to wait a long time before he got the engine started. Nonetheless, he rounded the block with two loud, victorious toots of the horn.

IT WAS DECIDED, I don't remember how or by whom, that I would spend the summer with him. And so, one day in early June, after a soporific passage through endless identical trees

aligned so uniformly you could look down the grid any which
way, diagonally or straight, my mother, who liked the declara-
tive as an expression of awe when confronted with objects of
monumental scale, pulled into a gravel drive and said, "That's a
mailbox."

The house itself was less impressive. It looked like a giant
had squatted on the roof. My father was waiting for us on the
porch. I have difficulty reminding myself now that even then he
was a young man. He was barely thirty. Today, when I picture
my father, what comes most vividly to mind is a disregard for his
appearance that I otherwise associate with the geriatric or in-
firm. The stains and mismatched socks, of course. But also: the
crust of toothpaste on his lips, the tail of hastily tucked-in flannel poking out his open fly. Although the sun was behind him
and we were parked no more than a couple feet away, my father
made a visor with his hand; he ducked and squinted. It was a sort
of pantomime, what he was doing—heavy, but he had a point.
My mother, who made no move to exit the vehicle, might as well
have been across a sea.

I waited for her to leave before I crossed the dirt and dan-
delion yard. When I reached him, my father was still scowling
after her departure.

"She couldn't even say hello?" he asked.

"Where's Lucy?" I said.

At last my father looked at me. "Oh, I see," he said. "Jim
killed the dog—is that it? Jim the dog killer? What else has she
been telling you?"

Jim was my father.

Without inviting me to follow, he went into the house. A
minute later, Lucy came plowing through the door. She seemed
skinny.

"Did you miss her?" asked my father. "I bet your mother says she misses her. But then, she was just here, wasn't she? And she didn't seem to want to see her, did she?"

"Hank got us a Doberman," I said. "A thoroughbred."

"What I would've given," my father said.

"For what?"

"To've seen her face. To've seen the look on Linda's face."

Linda was my mother.

After a while, I said, "What kind of trees are they?"

My father's shoulders rose and fell. "Walnuts, Kyle. They're walnut trees."

We sat on the porch. Still preoccupied by my mother's not getting out of the car, not saying hello, my father was in a grim mood. He clearly didn't feel like talking. I occupied myself with Lucy, picking a disturbing number of ticks from her hide, wiping the encrusted discharge from her eyes. The sun was starting to set—the shadows of the orchard creeping like a tar spill—when a faint rumble of machinery approached and I felt her tense. Soon, a six-wheel dump truck barreled up the road. Others followed close behind. They were big and loud and traveled at a reckless speed. Debris lifted off their loads.

"Gravel deliveries," my father said. "Turns out there's a quarry over there. Of course, Señor Esteban only showed the house when they weren't running." My father laughed, though not in a jolly way. "No surprise there," he said.

"Señor Esteban?" I said.

"Our amigo over at North State Realty." He pronounced "North State Realty" with a shrill, unrecognizable accent, intended, I gathered, to sound Latino.

"What about Lucy?" I said. She was still rigid, straining at her collar.

"She's got a cage."

"A cage?"

"A kennel. A pen. Hell, Kyle, you know what I mean."

"Can I see it?"

"Later," my father said. He laughed again. "Mexicans in suits! And I didn't know better?"

When at last we went inside, I learned the reason for his stalling. He still had not unpacked. The living room was full of boxes—some opened and rifled through, others still taped shut. My father stood amid the mess with his fingers laced atop his head. He looked rueful, and I felt he might apologize.

"A Doberman, huh?" he said.

THE CAGE WAS a cage: small and barren, littered with desiccated turds. That night I let Lucy sleep in my room. In the morning we were woken by the sound of my father's truck backfiring into the drive. I walked out to the porch and found him unloading several digging implements from the bed. A McDonald's bag sat on the roof. My father reached inside, underhanded me a wrapped McMuffin, and said, "There are things I haven't gotten around to doing yet—I'm aware of that." His manner seemed stilted, as if he were reciting prepared remarks. "The reason is my position at the hardware store," he said. "It's managerial. Managerial in the sense that they can't manage without me. That's how come I moved up here—the position. I don't know what Linda told you."

My father took a bite of McMuffin, chewed thoughtfully. "Also," he added, "what I said about Esteban? That was wrong. It's not a Mexican thing. It's any man. Don't trust any man in a suit. And I'm not just saying that because of what's-his-face."

"Hank?"

"I'm not just saying it because of Hank."

I helped him lean the tools upright against the porch. The

plan was to build a fence that would give Lucy the run of the yard. My father measured out the perimeter and at each corner held a stake in place while I sunk it with a mallet. He strung a length of twine between the stakes, and we went to work with the pickax and scythe. An hour later, when the brush was clear, my father hooted.

"Bring on the posthole digger!"

I approached the tools and reached for a heavy, beveled bar.

"Nope," my father said.

"Which one?"

"That posthole-digging one."

Grinning and wiping his palms on the seat of his pants, my father came over and picked out an unwieldy two-handled contraption with rubber grips and cupped metal blades. I'd rarely seen him so pleased. That grin! On the spectrum of my father's spirits, this was practically a manic state. "I guess Hank hasn't taught you everything there is to know," he said, raising the set high above his head, driving the blades deep into the ground. "I guess there's still one or two things you can learn from your old dad." He prized apart the handles and extracted a hefty wedge of earth.

"Can I try?" I said.

My father held out the digger. Without letting it go, he said, "Not too handy, Hank, is he?"

THE NEXT MORNING we visited the hardware store: a squat brick building with an old-timey parapet on a street so wide the cars parked perpendicular. A man stood behind the register, sorting through receipts. Squarish bifocals hung from his neck; a fat carpenter's pencil was lodged behind his ear.

"This your boy?" the man said.

"Kyle," my father said. "Kyle, George. You remember George."

"From the VA," George said. He smiled at me for half a second. "Cooper's birthday?"

"Hello," I said.

George returned his attention to the receipts. He used the bifocals like a magnifying glass, holding them by the frame just above what he was reading.

"We're picking up some posts," my father said.

"Took some tools yesterday?" George said. He dropped the glasses.

"Borrowed," my father said. "I borrowed a couple of tools, George, yes."

"Travis says the shed is half empty."

"Travis," my father said.

"Well?" said George. "You know the policy. Or don't you?"

The bell on the front door sounded and a customer walked in. George and my father both greeted the man good morning. They watched him turn down the plumbing and irrigation aisle. George said, "Can't keep making exceptions, Jim."

"This is Travis," my father said.

"Travis didn't take the tools," said George.

"Stop saying 'take,'" my father said.

"Take, borrow. Point is, there's a policy. Point is, the shed's half-empty."

"Jesus, George," my father said. "First you Jew me on my OT—now this?"

George glanced with alarm toward the plumbing and irrigation aisle. "What did I say about that kind of language in the store?" he said.

"OK, OK. But Travis—"

"Travis didn't take the tools," George said again. "And know what? Travis didn't leave the gate open. Travis didn't tip the forklift. Travis—"

"I'll tell you another thing Travis didn't do."

George held up a hand. "Not now, Jim, please."

I suspected that whatever George didn't want to hear about had to do with the army, Cooper, or the Persian Gulf, and I was about to make myself scarce when the customer reappeared and set two copper fittings on the counter.

"Get your posts," said George. "We'll talk about this on Monday."

"I'm off Monday," my father said. "Remember? My kid is here."

George dropped the fittings in a paper bag and told the customer the price.

IT TOOK US the rest of the weekend to set the posts, install the rails, the pickets, and fashion a gate over a footpath from the gigantic mailbox to the porch.

"I think she's got more room here than she did at Linda's," my father said as we watched Lucy get her bearings. "How about you?"

"It's nice," I said.

"Nice?" my father said. "She's got more room here, Kyle, by a long shot. There's nothing wrong with saying so." He picked up a rock and flung it across the road.

"Yeah," I said, "she's got more room."

My father spat. "Come on, let's clean George's goddamn tools."

———

THE LUMBERYARD SAT behind the store, a sprawling archipelago of building materials—pallets of cinder blocks and sandbags, stacks of treated pine, banded-together decking. When we arrived, a sinewy man in a hoodie was expertly handling a forklift. He darted here and there with ostentatious, adroit maneuvers. We parked outside of a low-slung shed, and the man zipped over, picking his nose with his thumb.

"This your kid?" he said.

"Do me a favor, Travis," my father said.

"George know he's back here?" Travis said.

"Will you do me a favor, please?"

"George says no kids in the yard, is all."

"Don't worry about George," my father said. "Don't worry about my kid. Just try worrying about yourself, for once, think you can handle that?"

Travis closed his mouth to swallow, after which it fell back open. Open was default, seemed.

"So this is your kid."

"Can you handle that?" my father said.

"Only telling you what George says."

Travis reversed away, forklift beeping.

The shed was lit by shop lamps spliced into an orange extension cord that drooped from the rafters. Steel racks lined the walls, loaded with cuts of wood. Between the racks stood the saws. My father ran his finger down the top sheet on a clipboard. He handed me a pair of safety goggles and bulky earmuffs. I could see that he was agitated; the encounter with Travis had upset him. Without a word to me, he leaned down and turned a handled crank beneath a metal table. A circular blade ascended through a slit. When my father flipped a switch, a motor jerked to life and the blade squealed into a silver blur.

"Stand over there," he said.

I watched him position a sheet of plywood so that it lay flat and flush on the table, and as he pushed the sheet into the blade, vivid yellow sawdust spewed onto his hands and arms, sticking to the hair. He turned off the saw.

"OK?"

"OK what?"

"Got it?"

He put a fresh sheet on the table, flipped the switch, and stepped away.

No, I guess I didn't trust him; I guess I never really had. Still, I slid the sheet toward the blade and was amazed by how easily it cut. The sheet advanced almost on its own, moved forward by the slight catch of the teeth. When just a few inches remained, my father signaled me to let go and pulled it through from the other end. He held up the bisected pieces, smiling. His mood had changed again.

We did a couple more cuts before the door swung open and Travis walked in. He took exaggerated notice of me standing at the saw, and then he said something to my father. I pulled the earmuffs down and heard my father answer, "Right now?"

"That's what he said."

My father turned to me.

"Don't touch anything," he said.

THE CUT WAS going pretty well, and I was feeling almost cocky, when I reached the last couple of inches, the place where my father had pulled the previous sheets through from the other end. Without him, the weight of the split ply hanging off the far edge of the table, tilting like a lever on a fulcrum toward the floor, caused the remaining uncut portion to ride up on the blade. I had to lean down mightily just to keep it on the table. The entire apparatus began to buck and tremble. The wood binding on the metal produced a strident screech—a sound that was altogether wrong. Afraid my father, George, or Travis might hear that awful noise, I gave the sheet a quick, panicky shove to end it.

A wailing brought me back. When I opened my eyes I was mortified to discover that it was me, those wails were mine. My father held me in his arms, squeezing a shop rag around my hand. It was wet and red.

George and Travis stood in the doorway. Travis somehow appeared equal parts triumphant and appalled. "I told him no kids in the yard," he said. "Damned if those weren't my exact words: 'George says no kids in the yard.'"

"Shut up, Travis," George said. Then he told my father to put me in the van.

THE BLADE HAD chewed almost two inches into the seat between my thumb and index finger, severing the tendon at the meaty base of the palm. In the emergency room, I was given Vicodin and told that because of the tendon an orthopedic surgeon would need to do the suturing. My father sat in a chair in the corner, caked with sawdust. A nurse brought him papers to sign. I felt I watched them from afar, and a tenderness swelled within me, a warm longing to close the distance between us.

"What about Mom?" the nurse asked.

"Pardon?"

"Were you able to contact his mother?"

"Do I need to?"

"Well, no. I just meant—"

"OK, then," my father said.

The next day, I found my hand splinted and bandaged. While

I was out, George had taken my father back to get his truck. As we drove through the orchard country, I gazed at the bucket on the floor. Inside the bucket was a pair of canvas work gloves, a plastic thermos, some hats, shirts, a leather tool belt full of tools, and a portable AM/FM radio with a handle and analog tuning dial. Even in my delirium I recognized the items. They were the items my father had kept at George's Hardware during the three-odd months he'd managed its lumberyard.

ONE MORNING A few days after returning from the hospital I woke and fumbled for the bottle of Vicodin, and when I shook two into my mouth I could have sworn that some were missing. My father was still in bed. In the living room I plucked a slice of pizza from a box and brought it to the porch.

Our new gate stood ajar and Lucy was nowhere in the yard. I called her. I was still calling her when my father came out.

"What're you yelling for?" he said.

"Lucy's gone."

He rubbed his eyes. He looked haggard.

"Someone left the gate open," I said.

My father sighed. "Let me get dressed."

We drove slowly up and down the long straight roads, shouting her name. My father shouted loudly and angrily. At a farm, a pack of dogs came rushing out from behind a barn; I saw the hope on my father's face. It wasn't far from there that we found her. Whatever had run her over must have been large. A good portion you would've had to scrape free with a spade. My father carried what he could to the bed of the truck. When he got back in, he had the smell on him.

He sat there with his hands on the wheel, and I figured he

was trying to formulate the appropriate remark. Instead, without a word, he started the engine and pulled back onto the road. He didn't turn around; he continued in the direction we'd been headed. I figured he was going to make a full loop of the orchard and circle back to the house—was wrong there too. At the next intersection, my father kept driving. We passed three, four more orchards before I understood where we were going.

At the turnoff, a No Trespassing sign was nailed to a telephone pole, and shortly thereafter the road descended abruptly into a gorge. As we made our way down, there rose a heavy clatter, metal belaboring stone. At the bottom was the quarry, a semicircle of sheer cliffs surrounding hillocks of broken-up basalt. Cranes moved material. My father and I were sitting in the truck, watching a backhoe scoop up a bucketful of gravel, rotate a hundred and eighty degrees, and dump the gravel into the rear of a six-wheel hauler, when a man in a blue hardhat appeared at the window.

"Can I help you?" He had to shout.

"I'm looking for the foreman," my father said.

"Steve? Steve should be in the office." He pointed at a mobile trailer raised on blocks. Then he said, "Maybe I can help you."

"No," my father said. "It's Steve I want."

He parked beside a motorcycle under a nylon cover and told me to wait in the truck. He walked up a ramp and into the trailer without knocking.

A few minutes later, my father emerged with another man in a hardhat. This man was older and wore a long-sleeve denim shirt tucked into dungarees; his hardhat was plastered with faded stickers. My father led him to the bed of the truck.

"That's your dog?" Steve said.

"Was."

Steve reached into his breast pocket and took out a pack of cigarettes. He shook one loose and lit it and returned the pack to the pocket. "See it happen?"

My father hesitated. "Yes."

"Where? When?"

"An hour ago. On Route Sixteen."

Steve inhaled a long drag. He stepped over to the window and grinned at me. "What about you, Bud? Did you see it happen?"

"Get away from him," my father said.

Steve continued grinning at me a moment longer, and then he moved back to my father. "Sorry about your dog," he said. "I don't think it was one of ours, though. In fact, I'm pretty sure it wasn't. Did you get a plate number?"

"Did I get a plate number? No, I didn't get a fucking plate number."

"Hey," Steve said.

Suddenly, the man in the blue hardhat, the one who'd directed us to the trailer, was there. "Everything all right here, Steve?" he asked.

"Everything's fine. Except this gentleman says one of our trucks killed his dog. Says he saw it happen. An hour ago. On Route Sixteen."

"An hour ago on Route Sixteen?" The man shook his head. "Wasn't us."

Steve shrugged. "Says he saw it."

The man turned to my father. "Get a plate number?"

My father had that look on his face. I knew that anything could happen. He said, "My son loved that dog."

Steve didn't seem to hear. He was preoccupied with the backhoe, which had just dropped its last bucket of gravel into the hauler. He signaled to the driver, who put the hauler in gear and began the steep climb up out of the quarry.

The man in the blue hardhat said, "Let's say you're right. You're not. But let's just say. What do you want? What did you come here hoping to get?"

My father started to say something but stopped. The two men waited. Even Steve seemed interested now. It was an interesting question.

I was sure that my father would berate or threaten them, spit at them, hit them, murder them. Any of that would have surprised me less than what he did do, which was mutter something I couldn't hear and get back in the truck.

George's was the only hardware store in town. We had to drive all the way to Sacramento to buy a shovel.

THIS ALL HAPPENED in the summer of 2001. I saw my father one more time, and then I never saw him again. It was December, a few weeks after he'd re-enlisted. I'd had a feeling he was going to do it. He was still living up there in the orchard country, but to no purpose. He was unemployed; he'd defaulted on his mortgage; my mother had forbidden future visits. On the phone he often sounded drunk.

That changed after the attack. The attack revitalized my father. As soon as it looked like there would be a war, war was all he talked about.

"Comes a point you can't keep pretending the world isn't what it is," he told me on the phone. "Sure, maybe Linda can, Hank can. But some of us know better. Some of us don't have that luxury."

We met at a Denny's, near the onramp to the freeway. My mother and Hank Rubin waited in the Jeep. ("We'll be right here, if you need us," Hank said.) My hand had healed. When I spread it on the counter to show him the scar, my father made as if to touch it. Then he stopped himself, smiled, and began talking excitedly about Fort Bragg. That was the base in North Carolina he was bound for, the same one he'd been stationed at when he deployed for Desert Storm. I listened with amazement. It was true: my father was going back. Not just back to Bragg and the army and the war, but back to the life he had lived before he met my mother, and before I was born.

He propped his elbows on the counter and held his sandwich in front of him. "I'm gonna take you somewhere when you come visit me," he said. "A restaurant. You go in there and it's Joes wall to wall, not a civilian in the place. They got a dish there. This dish is the best dish you've ever tasted."

"What is it?"

"The cook's been making it his whole life. His father made it before him—*his* father before *him*."

"What is it?"

"First and only time I've gone into a kitchen to pay my compliments. I was just a private, fresh out of basic. 'Keith, I would like to shake your hand.' That's what I said when I went into the kitchen. 'Keith, I would like to shake your hand.'"

"Who's Keith?"

"I thought it was the cook. That's what the place is called—Keith's." My father took a bite of sandwich, chewed, swallowed. He sipped his Coke. "Of course, Keith was the grandfather, the original cook. This cook's name was Clyde. Keith's grandson."

"So what's this dish?"

"Good old Clyde," my father said.

I swiveled on my stool to face him.

He smiled. "Sea bass," he said.

"Sea bass."

"You just wait," my father said.

NEW GUIDANCE

THE NEW GUIDANCE WAS: NO MORE AIR.

No more planes or helos. No more drones. No more Hellfire missiles, Hydra rockets, chain guns. No more evacs. No more rescue.

I was interpreting for Major Karzowsky and Sergeant First Class Boyle, who sat on the barracks floor across from Lieutenant Mustafa. The platters of rice and stewed goat had been cleared away; one of Mustafa's boys had brought in a plastic tray with a thermos, glasses, individually wrapped caramels, and a box of sugar cubes. The glasses, like everything else in Dahana, were glazed with an opaque film—what the Americans called "moon dust." Mustafa rinsed them by swishing a finger of hot tea in one, pouring it to the next. Meanwhile, Karzowsky and Boyle admired the artificial flower arrangement that sat on the metal filing cabinet beside Mustafa's cot. The filing cabinet was a holdover from when the barracks was not yet a barracks, from when the war had not yet reached Dahana. Mustafa had tipped it onto its side to serve as a kind of low-slung buffet. The flowers he had confiscated on patrol. Every plastic petal was a different color; at the end of each plastic filament an LED light pulsed.

"Do they want sugar?" Mustafa asked.

"Do you want sugar?" I asked.

Boyle took a cube and popped it in his mouth. He sipped his tea. That was how the sergeant ate: inserting one item at a time—a bit of mashed potatoes, say, and then, separately, a bit of gravy—rather than mix them on his plate. About this, Boyle was fastidious. The comingling of foods repulsed him.

After a polite attempt to sit cross-legged, Major Karzowsky had reclined on an elbow, feet out. He regarded his stiff, rheumatic legs the same way he regarded all disappointing things: as if they were his problem, not his fault.

"He doesn't look too concerned," Karzowsky said. "It were me, I'd be concerned."

Mustafa had produced a wrinkled pack of cigarettes, removed one, twisted off its filter, and drawn it across his tongue. He held the cigarette vertically, like a rose.

"That's his way," Boyle observed.

"What do you want me to tell them?" I asked Mustafa.

The lieutenant unplugged the flowers. Then he extinguished his cigarette, careful to preserve the unsmoked remainder, which he returned to the pack.

"Tell them their tea is getting cold."

ONCE, EARLY IN the deployment, back when the Americans and Afghans were still conducting joint patrols, we came under attack from a lone compound in a field. The Americans called for air; presently, two Kiowas appeared. The show was brief and loud and bright. Each missile sounded like a jet plane taking off. When we went to view the damage we found that the walls of the compound enclosed a small pomegranate orchard. Several of the trees were on fire. A motorcycle leaned on its kickstand beside a stack of poppy stalks. Chickens ran amok. There were two cows, and the front legs of one were a gruesome combination of mangled and gone; it was lowing insanely, using its hindquarters to push its face across the dirt. The other cow, or calf really, was still tethered by its rear ankle to an iron stake. The calf jerked against that tether with such adrenalized power it looked certain that something—the tether, stake, or ankle—would have to break.

I noticed, in the orchard, some of the Americans assembled by a tree. As I approached I heard laughter. The man sat in the leaves, his back against the trunk. A scrap of shrapnel had hit him in the brow. The crown of his skull had been sliced off. A flat surface remained that resembled one of those anatomical models showing a cross section of brain. The reason the soldiers were laughing was that someone had stuck a lit cigarette in his mouth, adding to the impression that, minus his exposed cerebrum, the man was just a man.

It looked funny, and I admit I laughed as well. I was still laughing when I realized that Lieutenant Mustafa had joined us. He stared right at me until I literally hung my head. Then he walked up to the dead farmer or Talib, plucked the cigarette from his lips, and ground it under his boot.

Thereafter, whenever Mustafa smoked in front of me—prolonging the elaborate ceremony: twisting away the filter, drawing the cigarette across his tongue, and holding it between us, vertically, like a rose—I understood that it was meant as a reminder, a rebuke.

A FEW NIGHTS after our meeting with Mustafa, Karzowsky suggested that I return to the Afghan barracks alone, to try to get a read on their morale. The sun was low. From the foot of the rise the company occupied, the country extended like an alien plateau. I walked down the hill, past the motor pool and HLZ, to the long wall of HESCO draped with concertina wire. The wall divided the outpost into roughly equal halves; the halves were linked by a heavy metal door; the door had a keypad with a preprogrammed code. All of this had been installed midway through our tour, during a nationwide rash of American fatalities at the hands of local forces. The guidance had come down, followed by the engineers, bulldozers, and backhoes.

I entered the code. Across the barren lot scorched by old burn piles, the barracks were still dark; the Afghans had not yet started up their generator. From the countless discussions about fuel that I had translated, I knew that Mustafa, ever since the Americans had cut him off, had been limiting his men to an hour of electricity each night.

The platoon garrisoned in an old USAID building constructed during the early, optimistic years to accommodate district-level bureaucrats. There was even a plaque, weathered and nearly illegible, something about "democracy . . . sustainability." The bureaucrats had never made it to Dahana, and now sandbags filled the windows, divots from high-caliber projectiles pocked the walls, the tables had been turned into beds, the chairs, desks, and bookcases used as kindling. At the entrance to the office in which the soldiers slept a door hung slantwise from a single twisted hinge. Black combat boots, stuffed with dirty socks, lined the hall.

In the center of the room a kerosene lantern sat on a stack of ammo boxes, hissing light. Rifles hung on slings from protruding rebar. The platoon was crowded on a plastic mat. Some were standing and others kneeling and others bowing. The soldiers with caps had turned them backwards. I recognized the orange-and-white one, with the Longhorns logo, that Karzowsky had brought back for Mustafa from his leave in Texas. The cuffs of Mustafa's fatigues were rolled above his ankles, and his bare feet glistened with the well water that he'd used for his ablutions.

I watched them for a while. Then I snuck back to my side of the base.

———

THAT NIGHT IN the D-FAC—a polymer shelter ventilated by gigantic fans, with neon lights and zippered exits, like the decontamination tent at the site of a biochem catastrophe—the CO demanded an accounting. It was Friday, lobster day, and yet each recessed division of Sergeant Boyle's tray contained a wet heap of peas.

"Peas," the CO said.

Boyle shrugged, and Karzowsky explained on his behalf that the sergeant found unpalatable the notion of seafood in a desert.

"Unpalatable," said the CO. "The notion." He wagged his head. "Fucking Boyle."

"What I tell him," Karzowsky said, "is a lobster has as much business here as the rest of us." The major gestured toward a private sitting at a nearby table. "He's Puerto Rican."

"Dominican, sir," the private said.

"He ask you?" Boyle said.

"No, Sergeant."

The CO was twisting a paper napkin around his fingers, one at a time, like he was getting off a ring from each. He frowned at me. "Muslims," he said. "They eat lobster?"

"Roo's no Muslim," Boyle said.

"You're thinking pigs," I said.

"Imagine?" said Boyle. "I'd sooner give up fucking." The moment he made the claim, he seemed to doubt it. "Now, hold on," he said. "That includes bacon—no bacon, either, right?"

"Got your turkey bacon," Karzowsky said.

"Imagine?" said Boyle.

"OK," said the CO, "so lobster they eat."

"I would," Boyle said. "I'd give up fucking."

"Be honest, now," said Karzowsky.

"I think I am," Boyle said. "Jesus, I am."

"Pork over porking?" the CO said. "That's what you're try-ing to tell us here?"

Boyle rubbed his temples, mulling. "We're talking I'm still married?"

The private at the other table smiled.

"Something funny?" Boyle said.

"No, Sergeant."

"Puerto Rico's laughing at my wife."

"If you're not Muslim," the CO asked me, "what are you?"

"Confused," Boyle said.

"Leave Roo alone," said Karzowsky.

"But your parents," the CO said, "they're Muslim?"

"They were," I said.

MONTHS AGO, WE'D discovered a large shed in the back of someone's house, the door chained and padlocked. We were sure it was a cache. But inside, instead of HME or Dragunovs, we found an antique dentist's chair, wood-framed, with velvet upholstery and a porcelain cuspidor. Shelves held pill bottles whose labels were too faded to read, dusty instruments, and sev-eral glass jars containing organic specimens of ambiguous prov-enance suspended in formaldehyde. Arrayed on a workbench were rusty scalpels and forceps, unsheathed hypodermic needles the size of bellows and turkey basters. Old blood on it all.

After facilitating an interrogation of the property owner—a "doctor," he explained, whose training had consisted of a month-long veterinary course in Pakistan some decades ago—I passed by the shed a second time and glimpsed something odd. A sol-dier, one of ours, was sitting in the chair. I knew him. He was a recovering crank addict from Georgia, Alabama, or somewhere, and he suffered from such horrific meth-mouth it looked as if he'd downed a shot of nitric acid and chased it with a pint of ink: all that remained were black nubs and splintery fangs clinging like a cancer to his gray, corroded gums. This soldier—I forget his name—was famous in the unit. He'd enlisted for the dental plan, so that he could get a set of teeth.

I stood there in the doorway watching him—he gripped the armrests of the chair, as if braced against the vision of his orthodontic future—and I was overcome with envy. Here was another one who knew what he was fighting for.

THE MORNING AFTER our discussion in the D-FAC, Boyle woke me just past sunup, banging on the door of my plywood hooch. I followed him to the tactical-operations center, a former clinic or courthouse that now housed a bank of monitors, like the flat-screen section in a Best Buy, displaying infrared surveillance feed from the tower, blimp, and drone. The CO, still wearing his workout gear—sneakers and a T-shirt tucked into aggressively short black trunks—was pouring coffee from an electric percolator into an insulated mug. "Get Mustafa on the radio, Roo," he told me, lifting his foot onto the seat of a pleather office chair, a kind of lunge position that hitched his shorts even farther up the thigh.

I glanced around for Major Karzowsky and found him leaning against the wall, a tumorlike chaw bulging in his cheek and in his fist a plastic water bottle half-filled with honey-colored froth.

"Platoon's gone," Karzowsky explained.

"Gone?" I said.

"Not fucking here," the CO said.

When I got hold of the lieutenant I could hear the rocks

under his boots, the equipment on his ammo vest clanging as he walked.

"Where are you?" I said.

"On patrol," Mustafa said.

"Where?" I said.

For several seconds, there was static. Then Mustafa said, "We're busy, Roohullah," and did not answer the radio again.

IT WAS ABOUT an hour later that they were ambushed. We could hear it from the outpost: faint reports from one of the insurgent-held villages to the east. Small arms at first—then rockets, machine guns, a recoilless rifle, and mortars. Eventually, out came the Dushka. When Major Karzowsky recognized its murderous kaboom, he squeezed his spitter bottle, making sharp crackling noises not unlike the distant gunfire.

"Guess they found what they were looking for," Sergeant Boyle said.

They did not return to base until sometime after dusk. They used their own entry-control point and went directly to their barracks. By the time Karzowsky, Boyle, and I got over there, most of the platoon was gathered at the well. A bearded soldier with a checkered scarf hauled a rope. At its end was a rubber bucket. The soldier used the bucket to fill several plastic watering cans. His comrades held aloft the cans, shut their eyes, and tipped the water straight onto their faces. They all stopped what they were doing to watch us cross the lot.

We found Mustafa with his NCOs, in the dim sun, amid a fleet of decommissioned Hiluxes. They formed a tight circle between the trucks. As we drew near, two of the sergeants moved aside to let us see. The dead man lay atop an improvised litter, tree branches run through the sleeves of uniform tops. His gut was an open cavity of gleaming pulp. I recognized him as a young private named Rahim.

Mustafa did not acknowledge us. Instead it was one of the sergeants who addressed me. "He has to go to Gardez," he said. "From Gardez, Headquarters will take him to his family in Jalalabad. Can a helicopter come tomorrow?"

The sergeant was an older, pock-faced mujahid.

I looked to Mustafa.

"Translate!" the sergeant said.

After I had interpreted the request, Karzowsky removed his ballistic sunglasses and clipped them on his collar. In this circumstance, he said, and in accordance with the previously elucidated guidance, the Afghans would likely be asked to bring their own assets to bear. Mustafa would need to submit an application for a helo evac to Brigade; Brigade would be required to obtain approval from Corps; Corps would have to contact the Ministry of Defense. Just articulating the process seemed to weary the major.

"This will take days," the pock-faced sergeant said.

"Why is he talking?" Boyle said.

"He should be buried soon," I said. I added, "It's a Muslim thing."

Karzowsky sighed. "Tell them we will relay those concerns."

"It's not up to them," I told Mustafa.

The sergeant was about to protest, but Mustafa restrained him by reaching out and taking his hand. As usual, Karzowsky and Boyle shifted uncomfortably; I too was unsettled. Why, instead of reproaching this man, his subordinate, was Mustafa placating him? Only later, in my hooch, did I realize that it must not have been easy for the lieutenant: persuading his men to follow him, without Americans or air, to that village in the east. No doubt the NCOs had opposed it. How had Mustafa prevailed on them? What had he said that night that I spied on the platoon praying together in their barracks? Whatever it was—whatever authority Mustafa had invoked or promises he might have made or point he'd been trying to prove—all of that was over now, as over as the disemboweled Rahim.

The following afternoon, the CO received confirmation that the soonest the Afghan Air Force could make available a chopper for Dahana was in four days.

BEFORE US, a Polish unit had the district. When we'd reached the outpost we'd found them in a state of siege. Karzowsky, Boyle, and I arrived with the advance party, a month ahead of the rest of the company, in the dead of winter. As our helo approached the HLZ, a chaotic gaggle of Poles came scrambling down the hill, slipping and sliding in the snow, inexplicably eager to help us with our gear. Later, we learned that the Wojsko Polskie awarded its soldiers additional hazardous-duty pay each time they ventured beyond the wire, and that the landing zone, though safely ensconced behind double-stacked bastions, technically qualified as such.

The *kapitan*, unkempt and possibly hungover, assured Karzowsky and Boyle that his men had been conducting presence patrols every day since day one. But when we met with the Afghans, Mustafa told us this was false, no Pole had set foot outside the base in months. Despite his effusion—he'd been stuck on that outpost with the indolent and under-resourced Wojsko for nearly a year, and he spoke now with the fluent urgency of someone who could finally be heard: how many more Americans were coming? what kinds of weapons were they bringing? would Dahana at last get the armored vehicles it needed? bomb technicians? air?—what I remember best about that initial conversation is that for most of it, as he talked and I translated, Mustafa never looked at me. Not until Karzowsky and Boyle stood to leave did the lieutenant abruptly turn and say, "And you? Where are you from?"

I hesitated. "I was born in Kabul."

"When did you leave?"

"When I was three."

Mustafa nodded as if that explained it. "Why did you come back?" he asked.

I was about to say, *Because this is my country* or *Because this is my homeland*—something like that. I was trying to decide what phrasing might be most appropriate when a rough voice behind me remarked, "What he means is, How much are they paying you?"

I turned and discovered several Afghan soldiers crowded in the doorway. They were grinning in an amused way; I realized they'd been there the entire time. In the middle of them stood the pock-faced sergeant. "Well?" he said. "How much did they have to give you to get you to come back?"

Mustafa rose and offered his hand to Boyle and Karzowsky. "The Americans are here now," he told the sergeant. "Maybe things will be different."

FOR A WHILE, anyway, things were. When the rest of the company joined us, the CO promptly established an operations tempo that afforded Mustafa and his men ample opportunity to exercise the violence—and then some—so long frustrated by the risk-averse *kapitan*. Back then, before the wall went up, I visited often with the lieutenant. He was friendlier than the enlisted soldiers, most of whom withheld from me the camaraderie they shared with one another as well as the deference they showed the Americans. Also, Mustafa and I soon discovered that we had something in common. Both of our fathers had been killed by the Communists.

Mustafa's father had lost his right leg to a mine while fighting Soviet forces in Parwan. When Mustafa was a boy, the flesh over his father's stump suppurated and became infected; he subsequently died of sepsis. Around the same time, my father, a professor at Kabul University, was arrested and sent to Pul-e-Charkhi Prison. We don't know how he died. Probably, he was tortured first. In those days, electrocution was popular, and ultimately, one imagines, he was made to lie facedown, shot in the back of the head, and buried in a mass grave.

My family fled to America shortly after. Mustafa's, of course, stayed. Mustafa's mother kept her dead husband's prosthesis in their house, propped upright against a wall, surrounded by candles, photographs, and fake flowers. Growing up, Mustafa told me, he regularly measured his own limb against it. When he judged that they were equal, he joined the army.

THE POLES HAD been receiving diesel via C-130. It had made you feel just how far away you were: those black barrels floating down, hitting the snow, sinking from view—their diaphanous, billowing chutes collapsing over them, enormous jellyfish landing on an ocean floor. The CO put an end to the airdrops, arranging instead for helicopters to sling in rubber bladders, suspended from metal cables, directly onto the HLZ. It was a regrettable coincidence that one such fuel delivery had been scheduled for the day after Rahim died; it was a potential provocation that a mail drop also had.

When that second bird touched down, its thumping blades raised a moon-dust pall so thick and high it erased the sun.

Crewmen in flight suits and white-skull face masks passed USPS boxes to a line of happy soldiers. After the bird was gone the rotor wash, like a foul miasma, persisted in the air; our ears kept ringing with its metal din.

"You think they noticed?" Boyle said.

One of the boxes, as usual, was for me. Inside was a pair of Gortex socks, some DVDs, and a bar of chocolate that had melted and congealed. A note, in English, asked when I would be coming home.

FOR THE NEXT three days, the CO banned visits to the Afghans. "Dudes are understandably emotional," he explained after Boyle and Karzowsky briefed him on the pock-faced sergeant. "And we're too close to home to let something retarded happen."

The night before the Afghan chopper arrived, I slipped out of my hooch, stole lightly past the tactical-operations center, and picked my way through the dark to the door in the wall. I entered the code. I stepped through.

The platoon was eating dinner, sitting shoulder-to-shoulder on the concrete floor around a rectangular cut of patterned nylon. Mustafa greeted me and made a space. One of the younger soldiers flung over a disk of day-old naan, and another pushed in my direction the communal dishes of brown rice, potatoes, and diced okra cooked in oil. I gave Mustafa the chocolate and the socks.

"From America?" he said with interest or irony, I could not tell which. He unwrapped the foil and passed the chocolate to the soldier beside him, who broke off a piece and passed it to the soldier beside him. The socks Mustafa tossed to the pock-faced sergeant. The sergeant immediately stripped off his green

Army-issue pair, which were full of holes, and put on the Gortex ones. He extended a foot and wiggled his toes. He seemed satisfied, and when he opened his mouth to speak I almost believed that he would thank me.

"This is what your helicopters brought?" he said. "Chocolate and socks?"

After dinner, Mustafa walked me into the hall, and then down the hall into the hot night. I thought he would accompany me to the door, but instead he said, "Come," and headed off across the lot. I followed him to the Hiluxes.

"We kept him inside until he started to stink," Mustafa said, reaching into a truck bed and unzipping the bag our medics had given him.

Rahim had begun to bloat and putrefy. His eyes bulged cartoonishly, his open mouth was filled with gray, swollen tongue. I had to pull my shirt above my nose.

Mustafa seemed unbothered by the smell. He held the bag open for a long time. Longer than was necessary.

Soon after that we went home. The company returned together to their base, and I returned, alone, to my apartment. All of my aunts and uncles wanted to know about Kabul. Was it true about the traffic? The Western-style restaurants? The compounds and the blast wall? When I told them that I hadn't been to Kabul, they became confused and asked, "Where were you, then?" When I told them about Dahana, they became more confused and asked, "Why?"

About a month after we got back I received an email from Major Karzowsky—an invitation to an awards ceremony at the company's home station. I packed a suitcase and booked a few nights in a motel room just outside the base. I was very pleased that the major had thought of me; I'd been growing anxious to spend some time with my old friends.

It was a four-hour drive through fragrant sunshine, wooded hills. The base had the pristine, landscaped feel of a college campus. Following a Xeroxed copy of a hand-drawn map, I arrived at a large white tent erected in a blooming flower garden. The unit was already in formation, the soldiers kitted out in creased slacks, gold-buttoned jackets, and black berets. I had difficulty recognizing some of them. Their faces were free of moon dust and fear.

I took a seat among the other civilians, the proud wives and parents, and we watched as the ribbons and the medals were bestowed. When it came time to honor the men who had died in Dahana, the CO gave a speech. He looked so much the hero in that getup, it was like he'd never had a choice. He talked about sacrifice, and soon after that it was over. People were getting up, hugging one another, leaving.

I looked around with a feeling of panic and was relieved to spot Major Karzowsky coming my way. He seemed surprised to see me.

"You actually came," he said.

"Of course. Where's Boyle?"

"Boyle?" Karzowsky glanced at a woman standing near us, rooting in her bag for Kleenex. "Let's take a walk," he said.

We followed a footpath that paralleled a newly asphalted road through sprawling lawns. Karzowsky explained that Sergeant Boyle had been demoted because of an "altercation" with his wife; the MPs had had to get involved. Then he'd gone and volunteered to fill a slot in a deploying unit—most likely, he was back over there by now.

Karzowsky told me about his new desk job and how much he missed being out with the grunts. I told him about the car I'd bought. Tractor mowers turned slow, broad circles, and the air was heady with cut grass. When, finally, I asked whether he had any news from Dahana, about Mustafa and the platoon, Karzowsky shook his head.

"Mustafa . . ." he said as if it were all so long ago only the name survived. "Remember how much he loved that hat I got him?"

"So you haven't heard anything?" I said.

Karzowsky winced, pained or annoyed, as if his knees were acting up again. I tasted bile in my mouth. I waited for the major to tell me what had happened. I waited and waited and then, as I waited, I realized I didn't need to be told.

On our way back, a squad of fresh recruits came jogging up the way. Their heads were just shaved, cheeks flushed, and their sergeant ran alongside them, calling out a cadence that they echoed in unison, with gusto. Before Karzowsky and I reached the tent full of decorated veterans and their loved ones, I had time for one more realization. I realized I'd been a fool to pack that suitcase and book that motel room. There wasn't going to be any big reunion.

PEACETIME

WAS LIVING IN THE ARMORY ON LEXINGTON AVENUE. First Sergeant Diaz had given me the keys. I slept on a cot in the medical-supply closet. "Two weeks, max," I'd told Diaz. But as the months went by, I kept postponing a reunion with my wife. I was comfortable where I was. The armory took up an entire city block. There were secret passageways, subterranean firing ranges, a gym with an elliptical. At night, if drunk, I connected to a bag of saline. I always woke up hydrated. I never had a hangover.

It was peacetime, more or less. It was for us, the New York national guard, at least. Between drills, I worked as a paramedic for a hospital in Queens. My partner on the ambulance, Karen, had applied to the police academy. She wanted to be a detective. This, for me, was troublesome: as a rule, from every residence we visited, I took stuff. Not valuable stuff. Small stuff. A spoon, say, or a refrigerator magnet. I'd never been caught. Still, ever since she sat for the civil-service exam, Karen had been acting leery. Once, while checking for prescriptions in a diabetic man's bathroom, I came across a plastic hand mirror, pink with black polka dots. I was about to shove it down my pants when I glimpsed Karen in its glass. (I brought it to my face, scrutinizing nose hairs.)

Often, when I got back to midtown, Diaz would still be there. Most nights, I'd find him in his office, updating his conspiracy blog. "Take a look at this, Papadopoulos," he'd say, turning his laptop around to show me a 3-D engineering schematic of Two World Trade Center, mid-collapse, with complex mathematical equations and swooping arrows indicating various structural details. "Huh," I'd say. Then we'd head to a bar on Third Avenue. Diaz, in his uniform, with his limp, almost always met a woman. The limp was gold. As the woman watched Diaz hobble back to us with drinks, sloshing gin and tonic on the floor, I'd say, "Fucking Iraq." She'd seldom ask me to elaborate. If she did, I wouldn't tell her how, as a squad leader, Diaz contracted a bacterial infection while masturbating in a Port-a-John; how the infection spread up his urethra, into his testicles; how that made him lurch, causing a herniated disk, which resulted in sciatica.

Instead, I'd say, "We lost a lot of good men over there." Which happened to be true.

If it had been up to Diaz, he'd have let me move my flat screen and futon into the supply closet. The problem was the new CO. After shepherding the unit through 9/11, Baghdad, and Afghanistan, our old CO, Captain Harris, had recently been promoted to brigade staff, in Syracuse. His replacement, Captain Finkbiner, was a former marine determined to show us guardsmen how a real infantry company did things. Finkbiner had the kind of face a shaved head did not flatter; the effect was less soldier, more chemo. Shortly after he assumed command, he summoned me to his office, and I had the momentary notion—seeing him there in Captain Harris's chair, behind Captain Harris's desk, wearing Captain Harris's rank—that he was a terminal case whose Make-a-Wish had been to be Captain Harris.

"Papadopoulos," he said. "What is that?"

"My name," I said.

"Cute," Finkbiner said. "So now I know who the joker is. The jackass. The clown."

There were no pictures of Mrs. Finkbiner on the desk, no

baby Finkbiners. The sole decoration was a large mammalian jawbone, like a boomerang with teeth. I barely glanced at it. With a weary sigh, as if under pressure to share a story he'd rather have kept private, Finkbiner said, "All right, Jesus, OK," and proceeded to explain that on his last tour in Helmand Province he'd been leading a patrol when a camel walked out from the trees. Twisting its neck, the animal regarded the marines. Then it turned and sauntered toward them. It was about halfway to Finkbiner when, boom, no more camel.

"Understand, clown?"

I smiled politely. In fact, I hadn't really been listening. My own thoughts wanted attending. Just what was the age limit for those wishes, anyway? Were there people out there, afflicted people, who'd missed the cutoff by a week? A day?

It was something someone should look into.

THERE WAS AN old Polish lady, Mrs. Olenski, who called 911 every Wednesday. She usually called during Tour Two, my and Karen's shift. I looked forward to Wednesdays: first, because Mrs. Olenski always offered me oatmeal-raisin cookies; second, because she was extremely rude to Karen. The ritual started when her husband died. They'd been married for more than fifty years, no children. After Mr. Olenski went, the empty, silent apartment began to harrow Mrs. Olenski. Only the television helped. She left it on 24/7, full volume; it made no difference what channel or program. It made no difference because Mrs. Olenski hated television. The advertisements, the laughter—ridiculous. Every time we showed up, she switched it off, massaged her temples with her knotty finger bones, and muttered, "Thank God." Then, as soon as we were out the door, on it went again.

Her standard complaint was chest pain. I'd sit her on the gray suede couch, pull up the ottoman, and go through the motions: take her pulse and blood pressure, conduct a thorough medical history, provide oxygen. Meanwhile, Karen would stand off to the side, refusing to assist. Her feeling was that Mrs. Olenski abused the system, exploited city resources, and that I, by humoring her and eating her cookies, was complicit. Alive to Karen's judgment, Mrs. Olenski directed all her old-lady kindnesses to me, sometimes ignoring Karen altogether, other times behaving toward her with overt hostility. Once, while Velcroing the BP cuff around her arm (on that arm, you had to use the pediatric cuff), I noticed her finger writing something on the couch cushion, smoothing down the nap. For a moment, I thought that she'd suffered a stroke and wanted to convey the fact to me. I checked her face for droop. When I looked back at the message, it read "whor."

Later, in the bus, Karen said, "You think you're being a good person, but you're not. What you're being is afraid. You're afraid that's you."

She was in the driver's seat, one hand draped on the wheel, the other gloved by a bag of jalapeño Combos. Someday, she was going to make a fine detective.

"You should lay off the Combos," I said.

"Don't cut my leathers," Karen said.

Don't cut my leathers. Years before, we'd responded to a motor-vehicle accident on the BQE. Law enforcement had cordoned off a lane. A snaking peel of tread led to a motorcycle wedged beneath the guardrail. A man writhed in a slick of blood. Somehow he'd managed to slide, rather than tumble, over the asphalt. Both buttocks were gone. While Karen prepped the stretcher and applied the collar, I got out my trauma shears. Until then, the guy had been only semiconscious, murmuring, in a daze,

"My ass, man, my fucking ass." Soon as I squeezed the scissors, though, he started, looked back at me, and said it.

"Don't cut my leathers."

After that, all the paramedics on Tour Two, and most of the nurses in the ER, adopted the phrase. Its meaning was elastic. I often invoked it when the supervisor made us pull a double. Other instances included the time we had to extricate an unresponsive three-hundred-pounder from his bathtub, then found the elevator broken; when a girl who'd stuck a Beretta in her mouth and pulled the trigger, her tongue stud having deflected the bullet straight down through the bottom of her chin, asked us were we angels; and when Karen, after a gas explosion at a textile factory, snuck up behind me, whispered in my ear, "I'm keeping an eye on you," and, actually, had an eye on me, on my shoulder, the nerve dangling like spaghetti. Some occasions, I didn't say it but I thought it. Take, for example, the September 11 Victim Compensation Fund requesting documentation of my alleged pulmonary disease, my wife suggesting I have a think about our marriage, or Finkbiner inviting me, with great ceremony, to touch his lucky camel jaw. Take me recalling all the homes I'd visited, the misery inside them, the knickknacks I'd lifted.

MOSTLY KNICKKNACKS. Every now and then I overreached. Once, at the Ridgedale Projects, we found a teenage boy in a hoodie standing outside a redbrick tower, wearing headphones and blowing bubblegum bubbles.

"Did you call 911?" Karen asked.

The boy shook his head. We'd already reached the elevator when he said, "Mom did."

On the way up, Karen said, "Is it your dad?"

"Sort of," the boy said.

A grossly overweight woman wearing a terry-cloth bathrobe over a diaphanous nightgown over a brownish sweatsuit greeted us in the hall. "Done it again," she said. We followed her into a cluttered apartment, where she began leisurely picking up toys off the floor, clucking with annoyance every time she bent over. Children watched an action film. None turned to look at us.

The man was in the bedroom, supine on the covers. He was unusually small—his underwear, which was all he had on, looked baggy, diaperish—unconscious, and experiencing severe respiratory depression. Every ten seconds or so, he'd snort a gnarly breath through his nose, a terrific snore. His lips were blue, skin devoid of oxygenated flush. The nightstand was covered with pill bottles: mostly painkillers, a lot of opioids.

"For my aches," the woman explained. "But did he think about that either?"

Karen went around to the far side of the bed with the O_2 and the oropharyngeal airway. When she planted her knee on the mattress to lean over the man, the mattress gave beneath her, billowing out in liquid undulations, lifting him on its squishy swell. Karen pitched forward and the water continued to glug from one side of the bed to the other, raising and dropping her, the man. Ordinarily, this would have been a supreme occasion to ridicule Karen; I was distracted, however. Among the pill bottles on the nightstand was a large fountain soda cup, no top, brown soda beads clinging to its waxed interior. Held down by the cup was a handwritten note.

"Papadopoulos," Karen said.

She'd managed to kind of calm the bed and was bobbing gently beside the man. I opened the drug box, prepared a bolus of naloxone, inserted the needle, and drove home the plunger. The action was almost instantaneous. While we were still trying to bounce him onto the backboard, the man began to gag on the airway and slap at the oxygen mask strapped to his face. By the time we'd transferred him to the stretcher, he was back in the world and not the least pleased.

"Why'd you do that?" he asked us.

"Oh, fuck you, Marty, you fucking shithead," the woman said, quietly, and left the room.

I rewarded the man with another hit of naloxone, which made him even more alive, even less happy. Karen was busy with the gear, and I thought for sure the coast was clear. It wasn't. As soon as I put the note in my pocket, I saw the boy. He stood in the doorway, watching me with a basically impassive expression. He chewed his gum. He blew a splendid bubble.

"Let's move," Karen said, and the boy mutely watched us wheel his sort-of dad away.

The note was all run-of-the-mill, derivative material. A lot of I love you so much, a lot of I'm so sorry. Still, after that day, I carried it with me everywhere.

If I drank too much, I'd sometimes knock over the IV stand during the night, inverting my gravitational relationship to the bag of saline. In the morning I'd find it jiggling on the floor, still hooked to my arm, full of my fluid. I'd raise the bag above my head and squeeze it in my fist until the whole pink cocktail drained back down the tubing, into me, where it belonged. I'd yank the catheter from my vein, sit up on my cot, stumble past the floor-to-ceiling shelves, enter the combination on the drug cabinet, and open her up. Typically, what I required was a vaso-dilator/muscle-relaxer medley: the former to stimulate cranial blood flow, the latter to break the grip of the savage claws sunk into my face, determined to unmask my skull.

Often, I'd cough. If so, I'd scour the shelves for something to spit into—some gauze or a sterile eye pad would do. I'd inspect the sample, a squashed bug on the white cotton, with satisfaction. I'd seal it in a biohazard bag. I'd write the date.

One morning, the supply-closet door opened and Captain Finkbiner walked in. I gulped the pills in my palm, then turned to face him. He glared at me, Finkbiner, in his manner. He appeared to subscribe to the theory that if you wanted to unnerve a man you didn't look him in the eye, you did the opposite: avoid the eye by looking at his earlobe.

"Papaluffagus," he said.

I tried to say something respectful. One of the pills, however, had caught in my throat.

"No jokes, clown?" Finkbiner asked.

"I was just doing inventory," I said.

"He was just doing inventory," Finkbiner said, addressing my earlobe as if it were a neutral party, sympathetic to his contempt for me.

Right then, First Sergeant Diaz joined us. He looked at me, looked at Finkbiner, looked back at me. He said, "Did you finish that inventory?"

It was Saturday, a drill weekend. Soldiers were trickling in from Brooklyn, Harlem, Queens, the Bronx. I folded up my cot and gathered the medical platoon in a dark corner of the armory, out of view of the grunts. Nobody wanted to be there. Specialist Chen had brought a Box O' Joe from Dunkin' Donuts. We filled small paper cups and discussed the best way for me to dislodge the tablet from my esophagus. Sergeant Pavone seemed to have the most experience. A girl with whom he'd once had unprotected sex had suffered the same problem with a morning-after pill. All day, Pavone had plied the girl with water and milk, hot tea, balled-up bread and honey. He'd massaged her neck, made

her hop on one foot, held her upside down, commanded her to
yodel.

"So what worked?" I said.

"Nothing."

"So what happened to her?"

"Who?"

"The girl."

"The girl with the pill?"

"Yes."

Pavone shrugged and sipped his coffee.

It was peacetime, more or less. At 1300, we had a domestic-
abuse-prevention training. At 1500, we had a driving-
under-the-influence-prevention training. At 1700, we had a
suicide-and-self-harm-prevention training.

"Look like you're doing something," I instructed the platoon
before heading to the bodega for milk.

"Like what?" Specialist Chen asked.

"Training."

When I got back, they were working on Harvey, our Human
Patient Simulator, a computerized mannequin that had a heart-
beat, blinked, and breathed. One of the new privates, an outdoorsy type from Long Island, was struggling to perform a
needle-chest decompression. At last, Harvey's torso ceased to
inflate. The private tried to make light. No one laughed. Instead, Sergeant Pavone articulated the elbow hinge and pressed
two fingers to Harvey's wrist, feeling for whatever widget was
supposed to throb.

KAREN HAD ACED the civil-service exam, securing a spot at
the police academy. Now, whenever we entered a crime scene,
she sized up the place, noting suspicious blood trails, signs of

struggle. One day, law enforcement received complaints of a man head-butting concrete walls in an alley. When Karen and I got there, we found an emotionally disturbed person keeping two officers at bay with sharp, deft karate kicks. He was well turned out for an EDP. He wore a tasteful suit, an understated tie, polished wingtips; every time he brandished a foot at one of the cops his pant leg hiked up, exposing colorful striped socks. The only sign of emotional disturbance was a purple hematoma from his hairline to his eyebrows.

"What do we got?" Karen asked, employing one of her favorite *Law & Order* lines.

"Guy versus wall."

Karen nodded. She was still nodding when the EDP, with remarkable athleticism, feinted right, rolled left, and sprinted by us, up the alley.

We got the next call twenty minutes later. The cops had pursued the man into a residential neighborhood, where he'd bounded through the unlocked door of a brick-and-vinyl-sided duplex. Seemed he'd made for the kitchen, extracted a chef's knife from a heap of dirty dishes in the sink, and slit his throat. By the time we arrived, so much blood had pooled on the linoleum, I could see my dark reflection peering up at me, Karen's peering up at her. The EDP had very nearly decapitated himself, transecting both jugulars and the trachea. The cops crouched over him, pressing red dishrags to his neck. Their sleeves were sopping. They looked relieved to see us.

I kneeled above the man's head, intubated him straight through the laceration in his windpipe, connected a bag-valve to the tube, and told one of the cops to squeeze it each time he took a breath himself. By then, Karen was ready with the dressings; when we tipped the man onto his side, however, a bucket's worth of blood dumped out. I mean enough blood to make a splash. It looked like we'd exsanguinated a pig or two. I glanced up, searching for a towel or fire hose, I guess, and that was when I saw them sitting in the dining room.

The dining room met the kitchen via a wide, arched doorway, and the doorway neatly framed the young couple, who sat across from each other at a square table. In front of each was a wineglass with ice water, and a plate of greens. A cube-shaped candle glowed on a ceramic plate. I noticed now the pleasant sound of jazz piano issuing from a stereo.

Both the man and the woman held rigid attitudes of astonishment. The woman had brought her hand to her mouth; the man had turned slightly in his chair. It was as if, by running into their house, grabbing their knife, and murdering himself, the EDP had bewitched the couple. I felt pity and a kind of kinship. That might as well have been me in there, transfixed; it might as well have been my wife.

The look on their faces.

It made me want to warn them.

A FEW EVENINGS LATER, at a bar on Third Avenue, First Sergeant Diaz said, "By the way, did you mail a biohazard bag full of lung butter to the PO box for the September 11 Victim Compensation Fund?"

"What kind of a question is that?" I demanded.

Diaz sipped his beer. He waved. "Never trusted that outfit. Follow the money, right?"

Not long afterward, the supervisor accosted Karen and me in the garage. "Either of you two take a snow globe from that house on Waring Ave?" he asked.

Karen said nothing.

"A what?" I said.

"A snow globe."

"A snow globe?"

"Homeowners claim it's missing."

"Guy practically cuts his head off in their kitchen, they're worried about a snow globe?"

The supervisor shrugged, checked his watch. "I said I'd ask; I've asked." He walked away.

"Believe that?" I said.

Karen was gazing at me sadly. "You need help, Papadopoulos," she said. "I say that as your friend, your partner, and as a future law-enforcement officer."

I barely heard her. It was Wednesday—I was thinking about Mrs. Olenski, her cookies. Olenski, however, didn't call. She didn't call the next Wednesday either, or the one after that. Finally, I suggested we stop by, and Karen, her investigative instincts eclipsing her dislike, allowed, "Something doesn't smell right."

Prescient words.

The stench reached into the hall. The TV was on. Through the walls, we could hear Rod Roddy urging someone to come on down. Fire joined us. Police. When they jimmied the door, we found Mrs. Olenski rotting on the couch, remote control in her translucent hand.

While Karen chatted with the cops, musing on the possibility of foul play, I wandered down the hall, into the bedroom. The bed was elaborately made; against the headboard, lace pillows were stacked in order of descending size, from enormous to tiny. By the window, a long-handled shoehorn leaned against a wicker chair, and several pairs of what must have been Mr. Olenski's shoes, thick-soled loafers and white orthopedic sneakers, warmed near an electric heater. I went to the bureau and opened the drawers. I peeked in the bathroom. I checked the closet. Karen was calling. "Just a minute!" I shouted. What was I looking for? I was about to leave when I noticed, there on the nightstand, the dentures soaking in a glass of water.

NEXT DRILL WEEKEND, Finkbiner was on the warpath. Seemed somebody had stolen his mandible. I corralled the platoon in the medical-supply closet and shut the door. "Get comfortable," I told them. We sat on ammo boxes, cots, and totes, dozing and eating the everything bagels Specialist Chen had brought. At some point, the private from Long Island, the one who'd let Harvey die, asked Sergeant Pavone, "What's the worst, craziest, most fucked-up thing you ever saw?" And Sergeant Pavone (whose two best friends had been crossing a bridge when an RPG engulfed their Humvee in flames and knocked it into the river—who, after learning that their skin had been charred and their lungs filled with water, had asked me, over and over, with a kind of awe, "Burned *and* drowned?") said, "Your mother's box."

I lay down on the floor and fell asleep. When I woke, it was to laughter. The private from Long Island had something in his hand. A set of teeth. The private was clacking them. As I sat up, the private aimed the teeth at me, clacked them, and barked. I must not have looked amused. The laughter stopped; Pavone cleared his throat. "Are they yours, Sergeant?" the private asked.

I lay back down. I went back to sleep.

MY TIME AT the armory was coming to an end. After the jaw-bone disappeared, Finkbiner bought a surveillance camera. He informed Diaz, who informed me, that it would be installed the following week.

The house where my wife lived—where we had lived together—was two trains and a short bus ride away. I found Elijah, our neighbor, exactly as I'd left him: shoulder-deep in the engine of his Chevy, defiantly exhibiting his bottom. When he saw me, he straightened. "Back from the dead," he said, dragging two black palm prints across his tank top.

I waved and kept moving. When I got to our door, I was surprised to find it padlocked with a heavy steel latch. I lifted the mail slot and peered inside. Another surprise. All the furniture was gone, the living room empty. A few packing peanuts were scattered on the floor; a bulbless lamp stood unplugged.

Elijah was out on the sidewalk, a wrench in his hand, watching me. I walked back to him.

"Where'd she go?" I said.

"Arizona. Nevada. Someplace like that."

"Why?"

"Mike had another opportunity, a fellowship or grant or something." Elijah tapped his brow with the wrench. "Sharp, that Mike. A genius, if you ask me."

"Who's Mike?" I said.

"You know," Elijah said. "Mike."

I thought about that. "When'd they leave?"

"Four, five months ago?" Elijah cocked his head and squinted at me. "So, what, you get sent over there again? I thought we were done with all that."

"We are," I said.

Elijah nodded. "About time," he said. Then he frowned in a serious way and extended his greasy hand. I took it. "Welcome home," Elijah said.

———

It was Karen's last month on the bus, her last month as a paramedic. No, I was not happy for her. Every chance I got, I cut her leathers. "Did I ever tell you about Jim Volkmann?" I said. Jim Volkmann was regular army. He died in Baghdad, in my arms, two weeks before the end of his tour. "Look," I said, pulling out the dog tag I'd taken from Jim's chain. (Understandably, Karen was unimpressed: it was literally a dog tag—shaped like a bone, with the name Lucy engraved on it.) "Did I ever tell you about Freddy Nevins?" I said. Freddy Nevins, like me, had joined the national guard when it was still the national guard: adult Boy Scouts, money for college, a reprieve from the city one weekend a month. On the last day of our last deployment, Nevins was in the turret of an MRAP, climbing a small hill to bid farewell to the Afghan Army soldiers who manned the observation post on top. A high-voltage, low-hanging electrical wire caught Nevins right between his flak and Kevlar, right where it could kill him.

"Just saying," I told Karen.

She smiled. You couldn't nick her with a chain saw. "I've heard that one," she said. "Only his name wasn't Freddy Nevins. And there were no Afghan soldiers. And it wasn't a wire."

A few days before her final shift, they sent us to the projects. I recognized the building and apartment number instantly. It was the small man: that fucking shithead, Marty.

Once again, the boy in the hoodie met us outside the lobby, and once again the obese woman wearily led us to the bedroom. She wore the same bathrobe as before, and the same nightgown—but her sweatsuit, this time, was purplish, not brownish. Little else had changed. The action on the TV continued. The children glowed on.

As I injected the man with yet another bolus of naloxone, I

looked at the boy in the hoodie. He chewed his gum, blew his bubbles, and said nothing.

En route to the hospital, I sat behind the man, monitoring his vitals. "Why'd you do that?" he kept asking. "Why'd you have to go and do that?"

After we delivered him, I changed the sheets on the stretcher and got a fresh backboard from the locker in the ambulance bay. I took out my wallet. I felt the note. I rubbed the paper between my thumb and finger. I brought the paper out. I smelled it. I unfolded it. I was just about to read it—I don't know, I wanted to read it—when Karen, wild-eyed, hopped down from the back of the bus.

"Where's the drug box?" she said.

NOT UNTIL WE were racing back to Ridgedale did the full magnitude of my blunder begin to impress itself on me. There were enough narcotics in that box to put a family down. There were nerve agents, paralytic agents, anti-arrhythmic agents. There were vials of pure adrenaline, sedatives, steroids, Valium, and anesthetics.

"That boy," I said. "I was distracted."

Karen switched on the lights and siren. She clenched her teeth. It looked like a mini tachycardic heart was galloping in her cheek. "My last month," she said.

When we got there, Karen stayed in the bus while I ran inside. The sweatsuited woman crossed her arms and clucked while I searched the bedroom. "You people," she commented. The box wasn't there.

When I asked her where her son was, the woman scowled and reared back, as if from a bee.

Karen was waiting in the lobby.

"I'm calling it in," she said.

"Nobody's calling anybody," I said.

I walked outside. The light was dimming, and the lamps, in anticipation, were on. I followed a footpath, distended by shallow tree roots, around the corner. In the lamp-and-evening light I saw a small playground: a metal climbing structure and a swing set anchored to a concrete pad. A group of teenagers were gathered by the swings. They were huddled close together, convening over something. I approached with caution.

Before I got very near, one of them noticed me and alerted the others. There was some jostling—some hurried consultation— and then, all at once, they scattered. I saw, I thought I saw, a boy carrying something under his arm. I pursued him. We ran through the warren of brick apartment buildings, past more playgrounds, across a basketball court, across a parking lot, down a street, and then back into the warren, back to the first playground, it seemed, though maybe not. I had lost sight of him. I leaned against a lamppost and hacked up beautiful black samples. In the distance, a dark figure flitted by a window. I jogged there. In a lobby, beside the elevator, a door led to a stairwell; when I opened it, I heard footsteps and followed them up the stairs. I was so tired. I kept having to pause, slump against the wall, cough. At some point I realized that the footsteps had stopped. I opened a door, looked both ways down a hall. It was empty. I did the same on the next floor, and the next. Empty, empty. I reached the top. ALARM WILL SOUND, the sign said. I pushed and nothing happened. I was on the roof.

It was dark out. It was not evening anymore. How long had I been chasing the boy? I looked at my watch. Our shift was over—it had been over for some time. I walked to the edge of the roof. Far away, on the opposite side of the projects, I saw the blue-and-red lights of squad cars, the white beams of flashlights sweeping bushes and dumpsters. Beyond that was the river, a slick of oil in a phosphorescent sea. And beyond that? I closed my eyes, listening. Somewhere someone was calling my name.

A BEAUTIFUL COUNTRY

Z STEERS WITH ONE HAND. THE OTHER HE USES TO eat the chicken. For quite a while now, as far as Healy has been able to discern, the nest of old newspaper balanced on the console between their seats has accommodated bone and gristle, nothing more. Still, Z keeps finding bits to lower into his mouth. He lowers them, thinks Healy, as if he's both the baby and the mamma bird.

"I love chicken," Z says.

"I see that," Healy says.

Z shrugs, rolls down his window an inch or two, and then, guiding the wheel with his knee, forces the glass the rest of the way, with both hands, like a climber hauling himself over a wall. When he flings the carcass to the wind, the newspaper bursts open and a long string of juice whips back inside the car. Z frowns at the stain on his tunic. "Look at this," he says. He nods at the glove box. "In there."

Among the clutter, Healy finds some loose Kleenex, but when he offers it to Z, Z makes a face. "No, brother. The cigarettes."

Drab chaparral flows by. Here and there a compound stands, a truck is broken down, a driver squats in a ditch to piss. On more than one occasion, Healy has heard white men and women call this country beautiful. Observing the scenery, he considers how he himself might respond if called upon to describe it. *It looks like God took a shit on a rock pile*, he decides, *and then God kicked down the rock pile.*

"I thought all soldiers smoked," Z says.

"I'm not a soldier," Healy says.

"But you were in the army," Z says.

"A long time ago," Healy says.

Z asks, "Did you know Captain Todd?"

"Who's that?"

"Captain Todd."

"I don't think so," Healy says.

"He was in the army."

"It's a big place."

"Were you Special Forces?"

"No."

"Captain Todd was Special Forces," Z says.

Soon they are in the city. Healy seeks out the gaze of random citizens, testing the efficacy of his disguise. Earlier, at the airport, after watching the other Westerner who'd been on the plane with him get into an armored SUV escorted by hulking mercenaries with flak jackets and assault rifles, Healy was surprised when Z offered him the prayer cap, the neatly folded robes, and the camel-hair shawl. He was surprised when Z led him past the VIP parking lot to the scrum of local taxis, rickshaws, and this ridiculous Corolla. And he was surprised, yet again, when Z told him that his weapon would be issued at the base; until then they would be traveling unarmed.

That was three of them, surprises, before they'd even started. Now Z says, "We have to make a stop," and pulls alongside a long row of blast wall.

"What for?" Healy says.

"It won't take long."

A heavy steel bar and two policemen with Kalashnikovs guard the entrance. One of the policemen approaches the driver's side and Z has to repeat the project of getting the window down. After a brief exchange, none of which Healy understands, the policeman beckons his comrade, who inspects the undercarriage of the Corolla with a convex mirror attached at an angle to a wooden pole: a giant version of the molar-checking tool dentists use.

The first policeman lets up the bar on a rope.

"What is this place?" asks Healy.

"Stay here," Z says. He parks and disappears into a tall office building with a turquoise glass facade.

While he waits, Healy tells himself once more what he told himself at the airport and on the plane and in the small Mediterranean city where he'd been staying for reasons he cannot adequately recall before he came here:

Go home.

Z emerges from the building with a black duffel bag on his shoulder. It looks heavy. He has to twist at the waist to swing it into the trunk. When he gets back in the car, Healy asks him, "What's in the bag?"

"That one?"

"Yes."

"Two hundred thousand dollars."

Healy looks at him. "What's in the bag?"

"I just told you."

Healy gets out, goes to the rear of the Corolla, and opens the trunk. The duffel is stowed underneath the floor panel, wedged into the cavity where the spare tire and the jack should be. Indeed, it contains a large amount of local currency bundled into equal stacks with rubber bands.

Back at the passenger-side door, Healy bends down and says, "Feel like telling me what the fuck is going on?"

"Salaries," Z says. "For the guys at the base."

"That's not in my contract."

"It's part of the job."

"Not my job."

"No?"

Healy quotes from his contract. Then he says, "Transportation of large cash sums through enemy territory in shitbucket Toyota without escort or protective equipment or sidearm or, hell, I don't fucking know, a knife? Not my job."

"You don't like my car?" Z says.

Healy straightens. He props his elbows on the Toyota's hot metal roof. All around him, bullet marks crater the blast wall. The concrete partitions were likely moved here from another location, where they had faced the opposite way. The marks on the inside of the barriers give Healy an uneasy feeling. It's as if someone tried to force his way out of, rather than into, the compound—as if the walls are protecting the world beyond them rather than the space that they enclose.

After a while, Z calls to him. "Should I bring you back to the airport?"

HE CANNOT EVEN say when it was, exactly, that he stopped going home between jobs. His apartment in the small Mediterranean city sits on the top floor of a four-story complex, midway up a steep hill. A strip of brass trim separates the orange carpet of his sleeping area from the warped hardwood of his kitchen area. He spends most of his time in the kitchen area, at a table abutting a window that looks out on what was advertised when he first rented the place as "expensive ocean views"—a translation error that happened to be more accurate than the intended "expansive." For Healy, anyway, the view was less a selling point than the small, family-run grocery that occupies the ground floor. Previous tenants had established a system. You placed a list and some money in a basket; you lowered the basket by rope to the street; you hoisted the basket up with the items. Of this, perhaps, at times, Healy takes excessive advantage. Days exist when the prospect of human interaction is so odious that he waits for the grocer to show his back, hurries past him up the stairs, and lowers down his list.

Weekends, on the streets below, protesters with bandannas tied around their faces erect potter-plant barricades, start fires, smash stuff. Police in riot gear advance in phalanxes, knocking people over with high-pressure water cannons. They send canisters of tear gas somersaulting down the sidewalk. The white, noxious clouds reach Healy's window, seep through the cracked glazing and the rotted frame, pollute his kitchen and sleeping areas. Even in the bathroom, a towel stuffed beneath the door, Healy's eyes used to ache and he'd retch into the sink. (The bathroom's is the only sink in the apartment and therefore not only the repository for spat toothpaste and beard trimmings but also baklava-begrimed plates, coffee grounds, and bowls of soggy muesli.) After his first stay, Healy bought a gas mask at the bazaar, with circular eye windows and a hose like an elephant's trunk. Now, whenever the marchers are attacked, he stands at the open window, in his underwear, invincible.

Last he heard, his wife and two sons were living with Frank Boswell, of Boswell's Boots.

THE EVENING SUN, hued and magnified, is the mouth of a shaft they are hurtling down, into a fire. Every couple of miles, the charred wreckage of an ambushed fuel tanker lies on the roadside like the cabin of a jet plane after a supersonic crash.

Otherwise, to the dun-colored sky, it is empty, dun-colored country, unblemished as a dun-colored sea. There are no check-points, no bases, no convoys, no war.

Z lights another cigarette and tells Healy that before join-ing the company he worked as an interpreter for a small Special Forces team led by Captain Todd. His eyes kindle. They dilate as if to admit more oxygen upon the flame.

"You wouldn't believe the stuff we did," he says. "If I told you, you wouldn't believe it."

"No," Healy says, "probably not."

After several minutes, Z says, "Those are his clothes you're wearing."

"Whose?"

"Captain Todd's."

ABOUT AN HOUR west of the city, they encounter a grisly scene: what appears to have been a head-on collision between a station wagon and a small passenger bus. How such a catastrophe could possibly have come to pass on this desolate road without bend is a mystery to Healy. Nonetheless, here they are: the long wind-ing skid marks, the bus on its side, the wagon crumpled up, glass and metal everywhere. The smell of scorched tread still hangs in the air.

Z slows to negotiate the debris. Behind the overturned bus, people sit on the hardpan, nursing injuries. An old man holds a bloody hand over his eye; a young girl cradles an arm that looks like it has two elbows. A crowd huddles over something writh-ing. When they spot the Corolla, the less stunned among them gesture frantically for Z to stop.

Healy starts to say something.

"I know," Z says.

In the side mirror, Healy watches an elderly woman step into the middle of the road and beseech them to turn around. Arms extended, she looks like a signalman marshaling a helo. She stays there, signaling them, until distance reduces her to a shadow, to a smear, to nothing.

"Did you see that woman?" Healy says.

"Back there?" asks Z.

"Yes."

"With the bone sticking out?"

"No."

"Not with the bone sticking out?"

"Never mind."

HEALY'S WIFE AND SONS stand shoulder to shoulder; Frank Boswell kneels before them. Each of their socked feet is snugly planted in an old-fashioned measuring device, the stainless-steel kind with lines demarcating sizes and half-sizes. Frank Boswell scoots from one foot to the next. He adjusts the bars and plates, ensures that their heels are firmly backed against the cup. Now and then, he lifts their arches to administer a playful tickle. Healy observes all of this surreptitiously, from a couple aisles over, while pretending to shop for himself. Eventually, his wife notices him, frowns, and whispers something to Boswell. Then all four of them—Boswell, Healy's wife, and Healy's two sons— turn their attention on Healy, visibly discomfited by the fact that he is watching them.

"Can I help you find something?" Frank Boswell says.

Healy looks away, focusing on the shelf in front of which he happens to be standing. To his surprise, instead of the new and fashionable Western-style footwear attractively displayed throughout the rest of the store, this shelf is crowded with

Army-issue combat boots haphazardly heaped together. The rubber soles are worn smooth, laces frayed, seams parted. Mud still cakes the toes; stains splotch the beige nylon and the cowhide. Healy recognizes some of the darker splotches as blood. Realizing that he is barefoot, he begins to try some on. He tries one pair after another, digging through the endless pile. But none of them fit him; none of them are Healy's boots.

It's with a queasy start that he understands whose they are.

WHEN HE OPENS his eyes, Z is staring at him.

"You were doing this," Z says, and makes a whimpering sound. He laughs. "You see? Like this . . ." He does the whimpering again.

Healy rubs his face. By the time he checks the side mirror—half expecting to discover the old woman still there, signaling—it's too late.

The Hilux whips into the other lane, accelerates, and pulls alongside them. Healy looks across Z, into the Hilux's cab, where a man with shoulder-length hair and black kohl around his eyes points a rifle out the window.

Z brakes and the Corolla jerks abruptly to a halt. The Hilux stops just ahead of them, perpendicular to the road. Now Healy sees that half a dozen men crowd the bed. They get up, adjusting robes, turbans, slung rifles, and ammo vests bulky with spare magazines. One carries a grenade launcher on his back; another holds a light machine gun and wears the belts across his chest like bandoliers.

Z says, "No."

As three of the men approach the Corolla, Healy pulls Captain Todd's shawl tight around his face. One of the men, the one with the machine gun, stands at the front bumper, glaring at them through the windshield. The two others each take a side. They move with purpose, an irresistible momentum. In the army, they had a term for that. The term was: "violence of action."

The man who takes Healy's side has a funny sort of beard. It is mustacheless, Amish-style, and it is orange. Also, despite the temperature, the man wears a down ski suit and a wool cap. He yanks open the door, grabs a fistful of Healy's robe, and drags him out. Healy drops to his knees.

The man pokes him with the muzzle of his Kalashnikov. He stabs the metal flash-suppressor into Healy's sternum. Healy knows what the man wants. He wants Healy to look at him. That is what you do, after all, when you have the questions and the gun. You make him look at you.

Healy pitches forward and lands prostrate in the hardpan. He outflings his arms. From here he can see underneath the Corolla to the far side of the road. Z is on his knees with his hands cable-tied behind his back. One of the men stands before him. The man wears loafers, the heels of which are folded flat upon the insoles. *Shoe-sandals*, thinks Healy. The undercarriage of the Corolla cuts Z at the shoulders and the man at the waist. Healy sees beads of green coolant sweating from a hose. He feels microscopic life moving in the dust beneath him. He tastes his mouth. He smells the sun. He hears Z beg.

EVERY NIGHT, WHEN he is at the apartment in the small Mediterranean city, Healy lowers down a little more money and hoists up a little more drink. The basket is not quite wide enough to accommodate a 750-milliliter bottle, and the grocer has to set it at an angle, its neck protruding. This means that the balance is off, Healy has to hoist with care. The grocer watches from below, in his hat and apron, hands on hips, head thrown back. Sometimes passersby stop. Everyone is waiting for the same thing. Everyone wants the explosion of glass. The feeling that Healy gets when instead the basket arrives safely at the window, when his fingers close around its wicker handle, when the grocer shakes his head and goes back inside, and when the disappointed passersby continue on their travels—that feeling is by far the best part of Healy's day.

Once, he remembers, he told his wife that the war was not a war, any longer, it was a racket. Like all rackets, Healy told his wife, it would end.

FEET MOVE, DOORS SLAM, an engine starts, roars, fades away. By the time Healy rises, the truck is almost out of sight. Z bends over the front of the car, raking the cable tie against a sharp edge of bumper. He looks up at Healy. There is a nasty cut across his brow, the work of a butt stock.

"They knew about the money," Z says.

Healy points at the shawl. "You can thank Captain Todd for me."

Z stands. He has unmanacled his hands but still wears a plastic bracelet on each wrist.

"Captain Todd is dead," he says.

Healy shrugs and steps to the rear of the Corolla to close the trunk. What he sees when he gets there makes his insides lurch.

"No," he says.

He rips up the floor panel. There, wedged into the cavity where the spare tire and the jack should be, is the duffel with the cash.

"Z," Healy says.

When he closes the trunk, he finds Z sitting in the driver's seat—sideways, with his feet on the road. He stares blankly, Z, at the desert.

"They took the wrong one," Healy says. "They didn't take the cash. They took my bag. My bag with my ID. We need to go."

Z doesn't move.

"Hey," Healy says, stepping into Z's vacant gaze, clapping his hands. "We need to go."

"Can't," Z says.

"Can't?"

"They threw it."

"Threw what?"

"The key," says Z.

Healy leans into the car and checks.

"OK," he says. "OK. Threw it where?"

Still absorbed by the vast and darkening expanse, the expense, Z says, "Out there."

NEVER BEFORE HAS Healy appreciated the light's astonishing complexity at this hour. It's as if the shadows of the bushes are more tangled than the bushes. Still, he knows that what Z is doing—crawling around on his hands and knees, rooting through the sand—is wrong. One does not recognize the thing by looking at it. Resisting the impulse to focus, one lets the thing announce itself.

"What are you doing?" Z screams. Covered with sweat and earth, he stares up at Healy from the chaparral.

"You won't find it that way," Healy says.

Z doesn't hear. "What if they took it with them?"

"You said they threw it."

"But what if they didn't?"

"You said that's what you saw."

"There was a gun in my mouth."

"No," Healy says. "The key is here."

Z resumes digging through the sand a few moments longer, but then he gets up and joins Healy on the road. He points toward the city, an unreliable hallucination. "I'm going back to the crash," he says. "Those people might still be there. They'll help me. I can pretend to be one of them."

"They'll help *you*," Healy says. "*You* can pretend."

"I'll send someone for you."

"You'll send someone for me." The emotion in Healy's voice disturbs Healy. His instinct is to cite a line from his contract. He tries to summon a relevant provision, the appropriate clause.

Suddenly, Z starts to jog away.

Healy watches him, stunned. He is a strong runner, Z. Soon Healy can barely hear the clap of his sandals on the asphalt. Then he can't hear anything at all.

Two hundred thousand dollars! Maybe that will be enough. In the incident report, Healy will say that the gunmen made off with both bags, and who in the company will doubt him, after the ordeal he has been through, the litigation he could bring?

He will go straight home—straight to Boswell's Boots. No more Mediterranean. No more hoisting up his liquor in a basket, standing at the window in his underwear and gas mask. To start with, a family vacation. Some remote and wooded place; somewhere by a river or a lake.

The sun has dropped away completely, and the temperature with it. Healy's eyes are tired. The chimerical hues of dusk will not stay put. In the distance a pale burn precedes the moon.

Healy thinks he sees its glow catch something in the chaparral. He scrambles down and falls upon the object.

What he discovers is an old tank shell from many years and wars ago. Inscrutable writing is engraved across the copper. For a long time, Healy stares at it. When next he looks up, he finds a pair of headlights that are far away but getting closer. They approach from the wrong direction. They belong to a Hilux.

Yes, they will return there, to that beautiful country, every summer. Without question, there will have to be a river or a lake. That way, Healy can teach his sons to swim. And then, when they're older, he will teach them how to fish.

All he needs to do is find the key.

VISITORS

I T WAS A FOUR-HOUR DRIVE, THIS TIME OF YEAR, FROM Grangeville to Kuna, and as usual it was dark out when Jeanne left the house. It was dark when she crossed the Camas Prairie, climbed the bald hills, and dropped into the astronomic void that was the Nez Perce valley. It was dark as she followed the moon, like a spooked shoal of silver carp, along the Salmon River; dark in Hells Canyon; dark all the way through the wooded gorges of Payete Forest. Dawn broke right on schedule, in Cascade. It revealed a wide plateau, lake marshing out to pasture, cylindrical hay bales, and steam lifting off immobile cattle. Jeanne unscrewed her thermos and filled the top. She cracked her window. During the winter, even here, in the flatland, there'd been perils. The peril of sliding off the road. The peril of some battery or engine trouble brought on by the cold. During the winter, each time she had reached the Idaho State Correctional Institution— each time she'd glimpsed the concrete complex, the razor wire, and the flags—the first thing Jeanne had felt, before the other things, was relief. Now it was spring. The way was clear. The air was warm. Jeanne sipped her coffee. Soon she would be there: sitting across a table from her son.

A few miles past Cascade, she topped a rise to find a vivified sky, a low bank of flame, black smoke. A man with a bandanna tied around his face stood in an irrigation ditch, using a blowtorch to ignite the brush. Gray ash stuck to the windshield and the Buick filled with a pungent odor of charred chokecherry and sage. When Jeanne emerged from the burn, she nearly rear-ended a flatbed inching up the road. She swerved into the other lane and pulled equal with its cab. A man wearing a John Deere hat and a handlebar mustache glowered down at her. Then he punched the gas, accelerating ahead.

Jeanne laughed and fell in behind. She was already thinking how she'd tell it to Rob. The mustache, hat. The translation of experience into relatable anecdote had become almost automatic with her. Throughout the week she collected gossip, committed to memory amusing incidents and things seen on TV. Some-times, worried she'd forget stuff, she took notes and reviewed them in the waiting room. The pleasure Jeanne derived from all of this was not unlike the pleasure she'd derived from selecting what items to include in Rob's care packages while he was over-seas. It was the pleasure of coming across something that made her think, Rob will like that.

That's what she was occupied with—how to describe the hick as comically as possible—when the flatbed bounced on a pothole and a split log was ejected from its load. The log turned slowly in the air, hit the asphalt ahead of the Buick, and launched straight at the windshield. It impacted with a crunching noise punctu-ated by the glass turning instantly opaque. Jeanne slammed the brakes and skidded to a halt. When she got out of the car, the flatbed was long gone. Someone was hollering. She turned and saw the farmer running toward her.

THE FIRST THURSDAY she'd gone to see Rob, almost a year ago, Jeanne had sat in the waiting room with the other visitors and realized with a start that all of them held Ziploc bags filled with quarters. By the time the young guard behind the desk received a message on his radio and instructed the visitors to follow him, Jeanne had convinced herself that the change was needed to use the plastic handsets that allowed communication across the soundproof glass. As she proceeded with the others through buzzing doors, down bright halls, and across a gravel and chain-link-fence perimeter watched over by armed men in tall towers, she imagined her handset clicking silent, a voice like a pay-phone operator's announcing that her time was up, Rob moving his mouth mutely.

In fact there were no handsets, glass. There was just a large open room with lime-green walls, octagonal tables, and chrome-metal stools. The quarters were for a row of vending machines that sold candy bars and pop. Cup Noodles and breakfast burritos were also available for purchase. A microwave sat on a shelf; next to it stood a pair of salt and pepper shakers. As the visitors formed orderly lines at the machines, Jeanne studied one of the printed-out "guidelines" in plastic binder sleeves duct-taped to the tabletops. *All custody levels allowed brief closed-mouth kiss and embrace at beginning and end of session . . . Held hands must be in plain view for duration of session . . . Children ages six and under may sit on offender's lap . . . Attire: conservative. No sleeveless garments, bare midriffs, scrubs, shorts, miniskirts, bare feet, spandex, low-cut and/or see-through apparel. Proper underclothing mandatory.*

She became aware of someone standing over her and looked up at a middle-aged woman with short-cropped hair, a leather jacket, and a T-shirt featuring a wolf howling at a full, yellow moon. "He'll be disappointed if you don't get him any snacks," the woman said. Then she set down on the table in front of Jeanne a shotgun roll of coins.

———

Although most of the glass was webbed and white, in the bottom corner remained a clear patch through which, by leaning over and stooping down, Jeanne could see enough to drive. As she approached the highway that would take her to Boise, and from Boise to Kuna, she had to steer by hewing to the center line. That was why she never saw the Idaho State Police car until it was right behind her, siren blaring. The trooper wore wraparound sunglasses and a black, flat-brimmed hat tilted at a steep angle like a drill sergeant's. "Mind telling me what in the world you think you're doing driving with a windshield like that?" he said.

After he had called a tow service, after the Buick had been brought to a nearby auto-body shop, and after Jeanne had persuaded one of the mechanics to drive her the rest of the way to the prison, she arrived to find several of the visitors getting in their cars. Others sat at a picnic table beneath an aluminum awning near the entrance. They often gathered there, the old hands, to smoke and talk before the long commutes back to the places they were from. Jeanne hurried past them, into the waiting room, and presented herself to the young guard behind the desk.

"Visitation's over," he said.

"I came from Grangeville," Jeanne said. "My windshield . . ."

The guard shrugged.

The visitors were still at the table when she came out. Jeanne could feel them watching her as she continued to the parking lot. She'd never exchanged more than a few curt pleasantries with any of them. All these months, she had kept herself aloof. She knew that she was clinging to a notion that Rob was not like their men, and that she, therefore, was not like them. She wondered how long that would last.

———

THE FOLLOWING WEDNESDAY, instead of lying awake, waiting for the alarm, Jeanne got in the Buick and headed south. She drove all the way to Boise and, a few miles before the exit for Kuna, pulled into a truck stop. An electric palm tree radiated in the night; the words "Traveler's Oasis" flashed amid its neon fronds. Jeanne parked behind a dumpster, away from the pumps but still inside the light of the sign. In the backseat she zipped herself up in Rob's army-issue sleeping bag. Several times she woke to the clank and rev of semis downshifting off the highway. Doors slammed and men shouted. In the morning she used the diner bathroom to wash and brush her teeth. There were no towels. After rinsing her face, she kneeled beneath the hand dryer and closed her eyes against its burning roar.

She had plenty of time for breakfast. She took a booth by a window that looked onto the ramp. A waitress about Rob's age, in a red apron and white kicks, poured her coffee. "Much farther to go?" she asked.

"Hm?" said Jeanne.

"On your trip," the waitress said. "Almost there or are you just getting started?"

THE WAY IT worked was, the visitors seated themselves on the east sides of the tables and then the shift lieutenant spoke into his radio and a door on the west side of the room opened and the inmates filed through. Jeanne always tried to pick the same table, in the corner, which she liked to think offered some modicum of privacy. She arranged the candy bars and pop on the metal surface. The inmates entered one by one. They all wore jeans, collared T-shirts, gray belts, and denim jackets. Some wore blue slip-on shoes, others heavy work boots. The shoes were provided by the prison, the boots you had to buy from the commissary. Rob earned fifty cents an hour mopping floors, but Jeanne was allowed to add to his account and always made sure that its credit exceeded his weekly spending limit. She enjoyed imagining the cart stopping at his cell each Friday. She enjoyed picturing Rob receiving its deliveries: instant coffee, Top Ramen, new socks and boxers. Proper underclothing.

When Rob stepped through the door, Jeanne experienced the same instinctive jolt as usual: a kind of momentary lapse during which the cognitive dissonance that normally made living possible—the simultaneous acknowledgment of his situation and belief that he would emerge from it OK—short-circuited. The man who approached her table was enormous. The denim jacket that looked several sizes too large on most of the inmates stretched over his shoulders. His head was shaved. He wore a thick goatee. When he sat down he put his elbows on the table, made a fist with his left hand, and stroked it with his right. He stroked the fist as if it were a nervous animal. He did not mention the previous Thursday—the first Thursday since the beginning of his incarceration that Jeanne had failed to visit him—but Jeanne apologized anyway, as if he had reproached her, and recounted the whole story of the flatbed and the trooper. When she'd finished, Rob said, "So, this guy, did they get him?"

"Get who?"

"The guy. Jesus. Driving the truck? Who almost killed you? Did they arrest him or what?"

"Arrest him? I don't think so, no."

"What do you mean no? He almost killed you, right?"

"Did I say that? I shouldn't have said that. It wasn't that bad."

"But it could've been," Rob insisted. "It could've been that bad, easy. Did the cop take a description? Did this cop even file a report or anything?"

"Well, I don't know," Jeanne said.

Rob clamped his mouth shut and leaned back in disgust. "Unbelievable," he said.

Jeanne changed the subject. "All week I kept having these thoughts. Another accident, the Buick breaking down, me missing another visit, you not knowing why. What would you think if—"

"I'd think you had something else to do."

"Anyway," said Jeanne, ignoring that, "there's a TO just up the road from here. So I drove down last night and slept there."

"You did what?"

"Slept at the TO. In the Buick. In your sleeping bag. This morning I even had time for—"

"Why would you do that?"

"I just told you why."

Rob glared at her. "That was stupid," he said.

"Stupid?" said Jeanne. "I guess I don't see what's stupid about it."

"See that man over there?" Rob said.

Jeanne followed her son's gaze to a middle-aged inmate with slicked-back hair, sitting across from a woman with a baby on her knee.

"That man stabbed someone with a screwdriver for no reason," said Rob.

Jeanne nodded, waiting.

"Walked up and stabbed him," Rob said.

When it became clear that Rob did not consider any further comment necessary, Jeanne said, "Speaking of screwdrivers, one of the curtain rods in the family room fell down. The thing pulled right out of the wall."

"The bracket?"

"The thing the rod sits on. Is that the bracket?"

The kind of physical deflation that Jeanne knew this topic would prompt began in Rob's fist and spread all the way to the wormlike vein pulsing in his brow. Home repairs. For the rest of the session, now, this is what they'd talk about. Brackets and rods and what tools were needed and how they were used.

TWO MONTHS AFTER he was discharged from the army, Rob punched Derick Leisure during a drunken scrap at the Blue Moon Saloon, inflicting a subdural contusion that, several hours later, while Derick was asleep on his parents' couch, resulted in a substantial enough accumulation of blood to asphyxiate his brain. Two months. Jeanne still had not acclimated to the daily thrill of having Rob around. Since that day, she had often considered how much easier it all might have been had she only been allowed a little bit more time with him—had that sense of fascination with his presence only lost a bit of its intensity—before he had to go away again. But also, she had come to realize that in some respects it was better to have a convict than a soldier for a son. At least in Kuna he was safe; at least from there Jeanne could be relatively sure he would eventually come home. It was a medium-security facility, and even the gang members—Aryan Knights, Norteños and Sureños, the handful of blacks who called themselves Crips—were above all concerned with staying out of max. That, in any case, was how Rob characterized the situation, and while Jeanne knew that the point was to reassure her, she could also sense that it was true: there was nothing in that place to which he was unequal.

She'd never felt like that about the wars.

THAT WEEK AT the Cash and Carry, the smaller of Grange-ville's two grocery markets, where Jeanne stocked produce and collected carts, she kept thinking about the inmate with the baby. She supposed that what Rob had been trying to tell her was that she was dangerously naïve, oblivious to the menace lurking everywhere, and it depressed her to imagine the world as he experienced it: a world in which any given person might stab you with a screwdriver.

The next Wednesday, at the Traveler's Oasis, she bought silver sunshades to fit behind the Buick's windshields. She didn't tell Rob—not that week or any of the weeks that followed. As the weather warmed, she left the windows cracked and grew to appreciate the truck stop's unique bouquet of tumbleweed and diesel. Awkwardly comported on the backseat to avoid the middle belt buckle, she slept better than she had in months. The coming and going of the semis, the hiss of their hydraulic brakes, the curses, laughter, and expectorations of the drivers—it all just reminded Jeanne how near she was to Kuna.

The visits, meanwhile, proceeded as usual: Jeanne questing after Rob, Rob eluding her.

Then one Thursday, during a session in late June, while Jeanne was describing her plans to attend a Fourth of July barbecue at a coworker's house, Rob leaned forward and interrupted her.

"There's something I want to ask you," he said.

Jeanne sat up. She waited.

"Do you ever see them?" Rob asked.

"See who?"

"You know who."

"No," Jeanne said, "I really don't."

Rob made an impatient noise.

"Sheila," he said. "Neil."

Not lying never even occurred to Jeanne.

SHE SAW THEM. Of course she saw them. There were only so many places to go in Grangeville. But then, there was also more to it than that. Not long after Rob had been transferred to Kuna, something odd had happened. Neil Leisure, who'd always done his shopping at the Harvest Foods—the Cash and Carry's competitor—had shown up in the produce section. Jeanne was organizing the bins. She'd turned around and there he was: the father of the boy her boy had killed. Having torn a plastic bag from the roll, he was struggling to part the wrong end.

Neil and Rob's father, Clayton, had been acquainted through the American Legion, and long after Clayton left Grangeville, Rob and Derick had played together on the high school football team. Although Sheila rarely watched the games, Neil made every one. He usually came straight from the airstrip, where he did something mechanical that left black streaks on his clothes. He brought his own lawn chair and sat near the end zone, away from the other parents in the bleachers, where he could smoke and sip from a plastic cup. Jeanne could remember Clayton once attributing Neil's unsociableness, alcoholism, and temper to "some real My Lai shit" from Vietnam. He often yelled at Derick and the referees, and Jeanne would never forget one particularly uncomfortable incident during which Neil had to be told to leave the field.

In the produce section of the Cash and Carry, as she watched his large, stained fingers rub futilely at the plastic, Jeanne considered fleeing to the storage room. It was with surprise that she heard herself say, "You got it upside-down, Neil."

Neil hesitated before looking up.

"Hi, Jeanne."

"Hi."

"Heard about Rob," Neil said. "Eleven years. That's a long time."

For a moment Jeanne didn't know what he was talking about. Rob's plea had come with an eleven-year maximum, it was true; the minimum, however, was five. Jeanne had only supported the deal because the lawyer had assured them, given Rob's military record, that the parole board would be sympathetic. For Jeanne, eleven had never been a real number. The only number in her mind was five.

"It is," she said.

"At least you can visit him," Neil said.

"Yes," Jeanne said.

Neil returned his attention to the bag in his hands, got frustrated, and balled it up. "Still," he said, "it's a long time."

He came back a couple weeks later. Jeanne found him perusing the lettuce heads. They repeated their stilted greetings—and this time Jeanne had the strong sense that there was something Neil wished to say. He gazed absently at the lettuce.

"Sheila's making salad," he explained.

More or less, it went on like that. About twice a month, Neil would betray his lifelong loyalty to Harvest Foods, and Jeanne would find him absorbed in the selection of vegetables or cereal or dairy, whatever section she happened to be working. Their interactions were always the same: brief, elliptical. Only once had it gone beyond that.

It had happened recently, not long after Jeanne began

spending Wednesday nights at the TO. She'd found Neil in the
condiments, studying the nutritional information on a jar of
mayonnaise. After she'd said hello, Neil had set the jar back on
the shelf and asked her, "Seen Rob lately?"

The question startled Jeanne. It was the first time since that
first encounter that Neil had spoken his name.

"I see him every week."

"How's he doing?"

"OK. Considering."

Neil nodded. Once again Jeanne felt that he was mustering
the nerve to tell her something.

"That's good," he said.

SHE DIDN'T HAVE to stay. She could have moved south—to
Boise or any number of small, perfectly fine towns closer to
Kuna. She'd only come to Grangeville in the first place for
Clayton and his Forest Service job. She had decided, though,
that Rob should have the option to return when he got out. She
knew that leaving would amount to a kind of admission, and she
wanted that choice to be his. She wouldn't make it for him.

ONE THURSDAY MORNING in August a woman Jeanne recognized entered the diner. It was the visitor with short-cropped
hair who'd given her the quarters that first day in the prison.
She wore the same leather jacket and under it a T-shirt with the
image of a buffalo silhouetted by a low, orange sun. She spied
Jeanne immediately and walked over.

"I know you," she said.

Without waiting to be invited, the woman squeezed into the
booth across from Jeanne, scooting toward the window with la-

bored, seal-like thrusts of the torso. Once she was ensconced and, short of a fire, there was no question of her reversing the procedure, the woman said, "Mind if I join?"

Before Jeanne could answer, the waitress appeared, raised her eyebrows inquisitively at Jeanne, and asked the woman what she wanted.

"An OJ, maybe," the woman said.

The waitress turned to leave, and the woman added, "Actually, you know what, how about one of these too?" and pointed at a laminated photograph stuck in a plastic stand behind the jelly packets and the ketchup. The photograph showed a handled platter heaped with eggs, biscuits, hash browns, and gleaming sausage links and patties, all generously lathered with thick sausage gravy.

"One Hungry Trucker?" asked the waitress.

"Whatever you call it."

The woman introduced herself as Valerie Powell, wife of Gary Powell, Inmate 9852. Gary was halfway through a six-year minimum for credit-card fraud. He and Valerie were from Bonners Ferry, way up in the panhandle, an eight-hour drive, in good weather, from Kuna. When Jeanne told Valerie that she was from Grangeville, Valerie said, "Grangeville? Aren't you a lucky one."

It had been a while since anyone had called her that. Suddenly, Jeanne liked the woman.

"You drive through the night?" she asked.

"Used to," Valerie said.

The waitress appeared, set down Jeanne's omelet and Valerie's platter, and extracted a mini bottle of Tabasco from the pouch on her apron.

"Never like the picture, is it?" Valerie said.

"What do you mean 'used to'?"

"How's that?"

"You said you used to drive through the night. You don't anymore?"

Valerie upended the Tabasco. "There's a Super 8 a couple exits down from here. Some of us share a room."

Jeanne guessed she meant the other women from the picnic table; Valerie, though, said nothing more on the subject and Jeanne didn't push. Later, when they left the diner, she noticed Valerie noticing the sunshades behind the Buick's windshields, Rob's sleeping bag unrolled across the seat.

"I guess I'll see you over there," Jeanne said.

"See you over there," said Valerie.

During the session, Jeanne was distracted. A few tables away, Valerie sat with her back to Jeanne, facing a wiry man with jaundiced skin and several missing teeth. The sleeves of his collared shirt were rolled above his elbows, the tattoos on his arms too faded to decipher. He and Valerie were holding hands, fingers interlaced in the air between them. It looked like Gary was a preacher exhorting Valerie to testify.

Rob turned around to see what Jeanne was looking at.

"You know them?" he said.

"I met her this morning."

"Where?"

"Here. They're from Bonners Ferry."

"I know where they're from."

"She seems nice."

Rob snorted. "You don't want nothing to do with those people."

Jeanne had not really planned on having anything to do with the Powells; Rob's scorn, though, provoked in her a defensive feeling. "Her name's Valerie," she said, "and she seems nice."

Instead of arguing with her, Rob turned on his stool again.

This time he continued staring until Gary noticed. What happened next made Jeanne queasy. Gary, the more senior inmate, a man Jeanne would have crossed the street to avoid at night, released Valerie's hands and averted his gaze, visibly unnerved by Rob's attention.

"*Stop it*," Jeanne hissed.

SOMETIMES SHE WONDERED how many other people, if any, he had killed. Just as he'd never really told her anything about his life in prison, he'd never told her anything—not really—about the wars. Still, even during that brief interlude after his discharge and before his incarceration, there'd been clues. His unsurprised reaction to the news of Derick Leisure's death; his maddeningly indifferent attitude throughout the hearings and the negotiations with the prosecutor; that terrible, capitulated way he'd held out his wrists for the manacles before being escorted from the courtroom to the van . . . All of it seemed to support Jeanne's suspicion that she was missing something. All of it seemed to suggest that what for her had been a tragic fluke, for Rob made its own awful kind of sense.

This idea—that Rob carried a burden of guilt and was therefore somehow *relieved* to have been formally charged and sentenced—accorded with Jeanne's conviction that he was fundamentally a gentle person. That despite all of the pretensions to the contrary, his had never been a soldier's constitution: he was not at all like Clayton.

Jeanne recalled, for example, Rob's reluctance, during the plea-bargain talks, to accept in principle the distinction between "murder" and "voluntary manslaughter." Recalled the lawyer citing the presence or absence of "malicious intent." Recalled Rob saying that his intent had not mattered to Derick Leisure, it didn't matter to Neil or Sheila. The lawyer looking irritated. Asking: "Was I wrong to assume you preferred to be charged with the lesser crime?"

"Of course not."

But it had been Jeanne who'd said it. What if she'd let Rob answer that question for himself?

SATURDAY, SHE WAS on her hands and knees, gathering the avocadoes someone had knocked down from her pyramid display, when a shadow loomed across the checkered tile. As soon as she stood up, she saw that Neil was drunk. He looked as if he'd just run a marathon—in his clothes and with a flu.

Jeanne dusted off her pants. "What's Sheila making tonight?" she said.

"Sheila?" Neil squinted as if trying to place the name. He was holding something—a shoebox. He shifted it to his other arm and reached back to steady himself. Several avocadoes tumbled down.

"Goddammit," Neil muttered.

"Why don't we go outside?" said Jeanne.

Neil followed her like a scolded child. Passing through the big automatic doors from the air-conditioned store into the blazing summer night was like transitioning between light and heavy elements. Jeanne led Neil to a bench underneath a bulletin board. The parking lot was crowded; more than one shopper recognized them, balked, and decided not to say anything. Gnats swarmed the lamps.

Neil balanced the shoebox on his knees, his large hands resting on its lid.

"Ever hear from Clay?" he said.

Jeanne shook her head.

"No idea where he's at?"

"No burning desire to either."

"He know about Rob?"

"If he does," Jeanne said, "it hasn't made him poke his head out."

Neil nodded and fell quiet for a time. Or not exactly quiet. Every inhalation sounded like a chore he was only half-convinced warranted the effort. He said, "You should see the way Sheila's gotten. All that woman does, anymore, is eat."

Nearby stood a miniature space shuttle with a seat for a child. Neil and Jeanne watched a young mother deposit her son and a quarter. The shuttle began to move in small circles on a mechanical arm. The boy tested the steering wheel and controls; realizing that they did not control or steer, he pouted sullenly while his mom talked on the phone.

Neil patted the shoebox. "I guess you know what's in here."

"No, Neil, I really don't."

He didn't seem to believe her. "Everything he's done," he said, "I've done a hundred times worse. Clay too, probably."

He handed the box to Jeanne. When she lifted the lid, she found that it was full of envelopes. They were all opened, all addressed to Neil, and all mailed from the same return address: a government PO box in Kuna. The top envelope was postmarked just a week earlier. Jeanne withdrew from it a handwritten letter that was several pages long. It was signed "SSG Robert Alan Dupree."

"It's Sheila," Neil was saying. "She found out and threw a fit."

"I don't understand. . . ."

She'd put the letter back in the envelope without reading it and started flipping through the others, a sick feeling spreading in her body. They were stacked chronologically, the envelopes, a new one almost every week. They dated all the way back to the

earliest days of Rob's incarceration, right around the first time
Neil had shown up in the Cash and Carry.

"It's Sheila," Neil said again. "She wants it to stop."

They were both looking at the letters. Letters that even now
Neil seemed to assume Jeanne must have known about. Let-
ters that contained more words, by far, than Rob had spoken to
Jeanne during all of her visits over the past year combined.

And they weren't about home repairs, either. She knew that.
They were about the wars: Rob's, Neil's, and Clay's.

ALL WEEK SHE avoided the shoebox. At first she had it on the
kitchen table, then she moved it to the top shelf of the linen
closet in the hall. Wednesday night at the TO, cicadas smacked
against the tubes; Jeanne lay awake with Rob's unzipped sleeping bag draped on her like a blanket. For the first time since
Neil had given it to her, she opened the lid of the box. She removed the pages from an envelope. She held the pages up. All
she had to do, to betray Rob, was read.

Someone was knocking on the window.

Jeanne pulled down the shade to find Valerie Powell standing
in the neon.

THE MOTEL WAS one in a row, near the entrance to the airport. Jeanne followed Valerie's station wagon as it pulled into a
parking lot crowded with rental cars, flanked on three sides by
two-story wings, a balcony running the length of each. Valerie
led Jeanne past a covered swimming pool and around the back
of the rear wing to a ground-floor room facing a concrete re-
taining wall. She inserted her keycard and opened the door on

two women sitting atop the floral-patterned duvets of a pair of queen-size beds.

"Found her," Valerie announced.

One of the women was much younger than Jeanne, closer to Rob's age, and sat cross-legged on the bed in plaid pajama bottoms and a tank top. The other was older, wore a cotton nightgown, and sat with her legs extended, her hands braced against the mattress on either side of her. She turned up her eyes without lifting her head, and smiled. The girl went into the bathroom without a word.

Both of them, Valerie explained, were also from the northern reaches of the state. Gloria, the older woman, was from Sandpoint; Stacey was from Coeur d'Alene. They'd all been carpooling for the past several years, along with a fourth woman, from Moscow, splitting the cost of gas and the room. The Moscow woman's husband had recently been transferred to Orofino, and they needed someone to replace her.

The toilet flushed and Stacey reemerged. "You're not a snorer, are you?" she said.

Gloria gave Jeanne a reassuring look. "You shouldn't sleep in your car, Jeanne," she said. "It's dangerous."

UNUSED TO SHARING a bed, she woke early. Watching Gloria, her thin frame and shallow breaths barely disturbing the sheets, Jeanne thought of all the nights, more than a hundred of them, that she had slept beside the Moscow woman, now gone. In the morning Gloria and Stacey rode in Valerie's station wagon, and Jeanne followed in the Buick. At the prison, after checking in, they walked together through the doors and down the halls. Eventually, along with the other visitors, they found themselves standing between two chain-link fences, one paralleling the other, creating a fifteen-foot gap between. For thirty seconds or so—after the outer-perimeter gate had closed and before the inner one opened—you were trapped. It was here that Valerie Powell looked at the shoebox under Jeanne's arm. Jeanne prepared herself to explain. Valerie, though, just said, "We'll see you next week?"

Stacey and Gloria turned to her.

The gate opened.

KIDS

B Y THAT TIME EVERY LOCAL KNEW THAT KANSAS—
the wide track of barren earth and upturned trunks surrounding the patrol base, where we'd bulldozed the trees
and razed the bushes to deprive would-be waylayers of cover—
was a no-man's-land across which, absent permission, one did
not proceed. Nonetheless, according to Dupree, the kid climbed
right over the berm of logs, which the bulldozer had pushed to
the edge of the clearing and the locals, accustomed to burning
dry cow patties in winter, had immediately ransacked, leaving smooth poles like driftwood heaped along a tide line. He
climbed over the logs, said Private Dupree, set down the object,
looked at the tower, and waved. Dupree raised his weapon and
peered through the scope. The kid was skinny, barefoot.

"But the object," I said. "The object."

"Like . . . a lunch pail?" said Dupree.

We were in the box, a converted shipping container that
served as our tactical-operations center, huddled over Murray,
the contractor from Raytheon.

"Show me Kansas," I said.

"Kansas, coming up," said Murray, toggling the joystick that
controlled the camera.

"Go get Sergeant Parker," I told Dupree.

"Ain't no lunch pail," Murray said.

I leaned to the monitor. There, smack-dab in the middle

of Kansas, equidistant between the logs and the entry-control point, sat a five-liter jerrican.

"Is that?"

"Ain't no lunch pail," Murray said. He chuckled to himself, and I could tell it was going to become a thing with him. Next time we heard gunfire on the ridge—"Ain't no lunch pail." Next time a scorpion skittered across the tent—"Ain't no lunch pail." Next time someone pulled a six-inch hair from his instant eggs or the helicopters strafed or a mortar or a ZPU round whistled overhead—

"Fuck's that?" Sergeant Parker said.

I preempted Murray. "Looks like someone brought a present for you, Bruce." Like the mustaches, using their first names was something the bomb techs did to remind everybody else that they were special. I went along. They *were* special. "Dupree says a kid just set it down and walked away," I said.

"And waved," said Murray.

"And waved," I said.

Bruce Parker scowled at the monitor.

"Empty, I bet."

But after he'd suited up, ventured out to Kansas, packed some C-4 around the jerrican, and uncoiled a detonation cord back to the ECP, Bruce had his game face on.

"Not empty," he said.

At first, when we arrived in the village and erected the patrol base, we traveled everywhere by vic. They were magnificent machines, a locomotive's worth of steel on wheels, the awesome apogee of our desperate, decade-old pursuit of superhuman invincibility. And yet: if you sparked enough potassium chlorate under one of them, the effect was comparable to wrapping a stick of dynamite in tinfoil. Within a month, I had the platoon moving exclusively on foot. An engineer with a metal detector would walk point while the rest of the squad followed in a line, stepping in one another's boot prints or tight-roping down a trail of baby powder. Tactically, single-file has to be the least desirable formation into which infantrymen can organize themselves. But we were getting blown up, not bushwhacked, so fuck tactical, was my thinking.

It didn't matter. Soon they learned to employ components with a low enough metallic signature not to register on our equipment—clothespins and rubber bands, entire trigger devices whittled out of wood—while daisy-chaining them together with lamp cord and speaker wire. Early days, before we gave up going into town, we traveled via rooftop, humping ladders to lay across the alleys like a bridge. That worked until it didn't—until they started mining ceilings.

We'd lost three men, all to bombs, before this business with the kid.

Corporal Kahananui had been killed just two weeks prior. Kahananui had signed up under the relaxed enlistment standards of the late-aughts, between surges, when the army was desperate for bodies and taking any man or woman who could fog a mirror. What I mean to say is he was fat. It wasn't his fault. He hailed from fat people—fat was in his blood. His broad skeleton, good humor, and squat neck all seemed specially designed to accommodate the inheritance. How he'd made it through basic was the subject of much chow-hall speculation. No way could he have qualified in the push-up, let alone the sit-up, let alone the run. Rather, some drill with a quota must have fudged his score a point or ten. That drill, turned out, did us a favor: Kahananui was the greatest, most casualty-producingest machine gunner I'd ever commanded. He'd fallen for the SAW the first

time he felt it chugging in his arms, spraying metal down the
range at Benning. Call it an affinity, like the fat kid who chooses
tuba. During a tiff, he could fix a jam, reload a belt, or jury-rig
a broken drum with hardly a hiccup in his surgically directed
devastation. He had achieved that intuitive communion with his
weapon that every rifleman aspires to. It was humbling—it was
truly a delicious treat—to watch him work.

Still, though: fat. And so, between patrols, I ran him ragged.
Suicide drills with a MOPP suit and gas mask; calisthenics in
a rock-filled rucksack; mountain climbers, bear crawls, cherry
pickers, duck walks. Kahananui welcomed the abuse—he gen-
uinely wanted to lose. At some point he started calling me
"Coach," an impropriety I allowed. You made allowances for
Kahananui.

Then one day I caught him skulking out of the supply trailer,
his cargo pocket stuffed with Pop-Tarts. I marched him straight
to the NCO tent, where we found McPherson, my platoon sergeant, reclining on his cot with a laptop balanced on his tattooed torso.

"Now on, Kahananui gets the radio," I said.

McPherson tugged off his ear buds (which, from his pillow,
continued to emit small sounds of screwing), that scar on his
face like a continuation of his frown.

"He's got the SAW."

I shrugged. "Tough titty."

The SAW, with a full ammo drum and all the extra rounds
Kahananui liked to carry, weighed a good thirty pounds—the
radio, with spare batteries and antennae, at least twenty. On top
of his flak jacket, hydration system, I-FAK, and Kevlar, it was a
load. But Kahananui, in true Kahananui fashion, accepted his
punishment without complaint, laughing with everyone else

each time he geared up, piling that massive kit onto himself, heave-hoeing, and lurching like a warhorse out the gate.

According to McPherson, that's what killed him: weight. The device had been buried under the doorway of a compound they were searching. Although three men had entered the compound ahead of Kahananui—the third man having been Private Dupree—it was set too deep for any of them to compress its plates, close the circuit, and ignite the charge. Only Kahananui was heavy enough. Later, while debriefing me, Sergeant McPherson said, "With the radio and everything . . ."

He didn't finish. Didn't need to. By the time the kid pulled his stunt in Kansas, I was sure I could sense it: a suppressed hostility disguised as the strict adherence to enlisted-officer etiquette, a respect that was the opposite of respect—no one calling me "Coach," anymore, that's for sure. I'd begun interpreting any friction, any hesitation or hint of dissent, as having to do with Kahananui. I imagined knowing looks behind my back, privates whispering in the tents, a growing camaraderie, among the NCOs, built on shared contempt for me. They were all in this together, was the gist—all lumbering through the same goddamn minefield every day, struggling to survive the whims of the same goddamn lieutenant.

I felt betrayed. Didn't they realize, big as he was, Kahananui might have triggered that mother walking buck-naked, hungry, through the door?

A few days after Dupree first spotted him, the kid appeared again, again put down a bomb in Kansas, waved, and disappeared into the trees. Bruce set the binos on the sandbags, pressed his finger against his right nostril, and ejected something from his left. "Why do I feel like there's a spring-loaded bar behind that piece of cheese?" he said.

"Sometimes," I offered, "maybe a piece of cheese is just a piece of cheese."

Bruce looked at me. By then, I was adept at hearing what people were saying without saying. What Bruce was saying without saying was: "Then why don't *you* go blow it up, asshole?"

KAHANANUI'S REPLACEMENT, a Specialist Feldman, arrived with the next resupply. McPherson brought him to the box, said, "New guy," and turned to leave.

"McPherson," I said.

He stopped. I thought I saw him sigh.

"That'll be all."

After McPherson was gone, I glanced from Feldman to Murray, who seemed as puzzled as I was. We were both trying to figure Feldman out. The shadow of a fully receded hairline encircled his pale scalp, and his face looked like something thrown against a wall, sliding down. He appeared to have had the wind permanently knocked out of him, an unsoldierly absence of any pectoral definition whatsoever. His nose was honeycombed with capillaries; impressed lines from spectacle frames linked his temples to his ears. I'd seen generals who looked sprightlier.

"How long have you been in the army, Feldman?" I asked.

"Six months, sir."

Murray let out a kind of disbelieving whoop, turned it into a cough. Feldman, who evidently was already used to having to explain himself, said, "I was a teacher, sir. High school mathematics, eleven years. If you want to know the truth, sir, the truth is I hated every second of it. Then my wife left me, took the kids. I'd always wanted to serve. It's always been a dream of mine. I thought I'd missed my chance—but when they raised the age limit . . ."

"Right," I said. "What's it now?"

"Forty-two, sir."

"Forty-two," I said.

"Good God," said Murray.

"I'm not that old, sir."

"No, no," I said, even though he could've been, even though forty-two would not have surprised me in the least.

"Anyway, here I am," Feldman said. He seemed as surprised as Murray and me.

"Here you are," I said.

In the dark, even with the goggles, you couldn't see the baby powder. Night-ops, what we'd do was we'd break open light sticks and pour the viscous fluid over cotton swabs. The swabs, in the green world of the goggles, would smolder brightly, like radioactive mice. Not long after Feldman joined us, we followed one of the engineers, Corporal Sanchez, as he led us into the green, one hand working the detector and the other, like a wizard's, sprinkling a trail of emerald luminescence for the rest of us to walk on.

Sanchez had come to America on giant tractor tires lashed together with rope and cable. Once, at Fort Knox, while we were waiting in the bleachers for our turn at the range, he'd told us how, after four days drifting at sea, as his raft approached the beaches of Florida, a Coast Guard skiff attempted to intercept him. Sanchez and his raft mates dove into the water. Sanchez could see the sand, the resort guests outstretched under colorful umbrellas—then he heard the high gunning of an outboard and looked up at a silver hull, a man in a life vest reaching to grab him. At this point in the story, in the bleachers at Knox, Sanchez held out his own hand, fingers splayed, and, after a brief pause, closed it in a tight fist. Just as the Coastie was about to seize him, Sanchez said, shaking his fist, a wave peaked between them, pushing the skiff back to sea and lifting Sanchez aloft, conveying him as if on wing to shore.

That wave had left Sanchez with a pretty fatalistic worldview, which was why he remained unbothered by the fact that after two combat tours he still had not been naturalized, and why he didn't mind walking point at night.

We worked our way through the woods, down the valley, and to the river, where a large compound, identified by surveillance drones as the site of frequent comings and goings, was suspected of caching ordnance. We were just about to breach when the new guy, the old man, Specialist Feldman, dropped his rifle. The clatter roused a pack of dogs, whose barking roused the cats, whose caterwauling roused the jackals—none of which was as jarring as what Feldman did next. What he did was whisper, loud enough for all to hear, "I'm sorry."

Back at the base, after we found nothing and no one in the compound, Sergeant McPherson took Feldman aside and spoke to him. Light was breaking. On my way to the box, I saw Feldman standing beside the entrance to one of the tents. He held his carbine high above his head, as if fording a river. To every soldier who ducked through the flaps, Feldman said, "I'm sorry." Around noon, I stepped out for chow. Feldman was behind the serving table, holding up the carbine. As the platoon filed by, heaping food onto their trays, he again told each of them, "I'm sorry." Feldman's arms were shaking violently; his face was an alarming shade of purple. A couple of privates ahead of me were laughing. They must have been twenty years younger than Feldman, at least.

"I'm sorry," Feldman told them. "I'm sorry . . . I'm sorry . . . I'm sorry . . ."

Eight hours later, he was back out there for dinner. It was an unfortunate way to have to introduce yourself.

In the week following the night-op, the kid returned twice more. The second time, I saw him for myself. Private Dupree was on duty again. He radioed me as soon as he spied him scaling the logs. I sprinted for the tower. The kid was smaller than I'd expected. He had to sort of hug the jerrican rather than hold it by the handle. After he set it down, he wiped his nose with his sleeve. I focused the binos. His *kameez* featured an intricate pattern stitched across its chest in white and gold. He wore a brown prayer cap. He waved.

According to Bruce Parker, the outsides of the cans had all been marked with soil. This would have seemed to indicate that the kid was digging them up. Bruce went on to argue, however, that it would be easy enough for a person to rub on some dirt precisely for the purpose of giving that impression.

"Mousetrap," Bruce declared.

I admit I was inclined to disagree. The kid, after all, was the only good thing that had happened to us since we'd arrived in that fucking village. Within the platoon, he'd come to be viewed as a kind of a win. Moreover, since Dupree had been the first one to spot him, and the only one who'd seen him twice, a degree of the kid's juju extended to the private. In our minds, Dupree was connected to the kid, and this connection was in turn connected to Dupree also having been the last person to walk through the last door Kahananui walked through. Via Dupree, in other words, the kid was connected to Kahananui.

It was partly for this reason that I asked Bruce to keep his theories to himself. Another reason, I confess, was that ever since the kid I'd sensed less resentment from the men.

Specialist Feldman might also have had something to do with that. It was as if, with so much enmity focused on the math teacher, none remained for me. Every day his difficulties seemed to increase. For starters, after the night-op, nobody called him Feldman; he was known by everyone as "Sorry." McPherson's relentless hard-on for the specialist further estranged him from the platoon. Once, during chow, I heard McPherson say, "Who let this fucktard into my army?" and watched him march across the yard to where Feldman sat alone with a book.

"What is that?" McPherson demanded.

Feldman pushed his glasses up his nose and smiled. Somehow under the impression that the sergeant's interest was genuine, he began talking with enthusiasm about the book, a history of Afghanistan, saying things like, "It's actually quite interesting . . ." and "Says here the mistake the British made when they installed the shah was . . ."

A few hours later, when McPherson had finished with him, I summoned Feldman to the box. He was sweating so heavily that the salt stained his uniform in thick white bands. I tossed him a water bottle, and he turned it upside down, bobbing his Adam's apple until it was empty.

"I guess it's not for everyone," I said.

"Sir?" Feldman said.

I waved in a general way. "Why didn't you go officer? You have the degree. Army needs officers. How is it your recruiter let you enlist?"

"I insisted, sir."

Over at the monitor, Murray shook his head. I tossed Feldman another water. "You were expecting something a little different?"

Feldman shrugged. He was reluctant to acknowledge how poorly things were developing for him. When I suggested that McPherson would back off in time, it was nothing personal, he laughed and said, "Beats teaching!" He gulped at the bottle, wheezing through his nose. "Beats my empty condo! Beats having to see Brad Drexler every day. Drexler in the break room, Drexler in the halls, Drexler in the—"

"Brad Drexler?"

Again Feldman laughed. "Nobody, sir. A social studies teacher. My wife . . ."

He was smiling in an ugly, crooked way, lips curled against his teeth, eyes wrenched wide. It took me a minute to realize he was trying not to cry. When I did I understood why Feldman so disgusted McPherson. Quickly, to avoid saying something cruel, I pointed at his rifle. "Just show them you know how to use that thing. That's all that matters."

Feldman's mouth remained twisted in its mocking rictus. When he replied, "Yes, sir, I'll show them," it was plain that we were talking about different people, he and I.

A FEW DAYS LATER, while we were alone in the box, Murray said, "When I was in Iraq there was this squad leader. Sergeant Walsh. Not my squad leader. Not even my platoon. But everybody in the unit knew him. Walsh was the darling. High speed, Ranger-qualified, born for the uniform. Imagine Kahananui not fat. That was Walsh. So one day Walsh and his squad are kicking down doors. They're in this building where every time we pass it somebody fucks us from the roof. They come around a corner—standing in the hall, minding his business, there's this kid. Young kid, like yours."

"Mine?" I said.

"Only no man jammies. No week's worth of moon dust on his face. This is Baghdad. Oh, and he's not carrying an improvised explosive device; he's got that going for him.

"So Walsh halts the squad. The kid, he points at one of the apartment doors. He points at the door, says something to Walsh, and then he runs away. Interesting. Thing is, we're talking early days—Walsh doesn't have no terp with him. But he thinks, Walsh does, There must be some baddies in there. Sure. Why else point it out? Why else run away?

"You know what happens next. It happens the instant they hit the door. Blast nearly brings the building down. Dude from the QRF told me a flying TV almost killed some bitch five blocks away. Walsh's guys? Our guys? Two of them are dead.

"Two guys in the first month of our deployment. Meaning guess what? That platoon had an entire year to get theirs. I mean these yahoos were notorious. Sure, maybe the lieutenant was a fucking psychopath. But still: it all started with that kid. Kid's what set it all in motion."

Murray raised his eyebrows.

"You're saying you're with Bruce on this," I said.

"Hold on," Murray said. "The story's not about the kid. It's about Walsh. Walsh had a problem. His problem was: he thought about things. That way, he was kind of like you."

That way, I thought. Not the born-for-the-uniform way. Not the darling-of-the-unit way.

"One thing Walsh thought about," Murray went on, "one thing he couldn't *stop* thinking about, was what if the kid hadn't set them up? What if what the kid had done was warn them?

"Good question. A few days after the attack, Walsh visits the terps. He finds their hooch, knocks on the door, is like, 'How do you say, "Don't go in there"? How do you say, "Go in there"?' He says every line he can think of, every possible thing the kid might have said to either set them up or warn them. But of course none of it is ringing any bells. It all sounds the same. It all sounds like fucking gibberish.

"OK. Night after night, Walsh lies awake, he replays the scene. The kid appears in the hall, he points at the door, he speaks to Walsh. Everything is clear—*too* clear—everything except when the kid opens his mouth, what comes out? Fucking gibberish. So Walsh, what does he do? He starts hanging with the terps. He starts taking lessons. He starts trying to learn the fucking lingo. Now he's *got* to know, right? It's like this kid's words, whatever the fuck they were, are the key to the whole shitty mess. Like if Walsh can't understand them, he won't ever understand anything. He figures, Walsh does, if he can learn some of the lingo, maybe then the words will come.

"Well, what do you think? We're getting contact almost every day, losing guys, and our star NCO, our main dude, is spending all his downtime with the *terps*? Nope. By the end of the deployment, nobody wanted anything to do with fucking Sergeant Walsh."

Murray turned back to the monitor and began fiddling with the joystick.

"That's the end of the story?" I said.

He shrugged. "I got out after that tour and started working for Raytheon."

"Jesus, Murray," I said. "You're telling me you don't know what happened? You don't know if Walsh ever figured out what the kid said?"

Murray looked at me and grinned. What he was saying

without saying was: "You dumb son of a bitch, of course he never figured it out."

THE DRONES HAD spotted more comings and goings, and we had orders to return to the compound by the river. It was daytime. Sanchez was working the detector. He was midway across a wide, dry creek bed when he got a hit. I pulled the squad back onto the bank, and then farther back, into a small grove where a spring fed moss and trees. While we waited for Bruce to join us with the robot there came the scream of a shell and its breathtaking thunderclap near enough to wash debris across our backs as we pressed into the earth wishing she would open up. Almost immediately a second shell impacted on the opposite side of the grove, and the panic, the awareness that the mortar team was adjusting in, arrived at the same time as a barrage of small arms from our six, the bullets so close we could hear them whining shrilly, vibrating the air.

We spread out, returning fire every which way, bracing for the next mortar round to land. Sergeant McPherson yelled at the men to identify targets, locate muzzle flashes, movement, kill holes in the compound walls. I took a quick inventory and noticed, among the frazzled grunts, one soldier lying comfortably in the prone, rifle propped on a log. He was scanning a distant stand of pines while squeezing off precise, methodical bursts. The unhurried way the soldier was shooting and reloading—the way, at one point, he expertly cleared a jam without removing his eyes from those pines—stood in stark contrast to the existential alarm taking hold of the men around him.

McPherson saw it too, low-crawled over, and shouted, "What do you got?"

To which Specialist Feldman, ejecting an expended magazine and inserting a fresh one, responded, "Two o'clock. Tree line."

Today, no matter how hard I try to transport myself back to that grove, I can't say for how long Feldman's little moment lasted. Half a minute? Half an hour? I suppose it doesn't matter. For a short while, anyway, the old man was doing what he'd come there to do. He was showing them.

I was so distracted that I didn't notice Private Dupree until he hollered in my ear.

"He's here, sir."

"Who?"

Dupree pointed at a patch of chaparral midway between our position and the pines. I raised my rifle. The kid was squatting in the bushes, eyes clinched, covering his ears. Clearly, he didn't want to be there. The little bastard must have been following us, I realized, ever since we'd left the base.

Before I had a chance to consider what it might mean, or to alert McPherson, the kid did a jerky half spin, as if an invisible assailant had whipped him around from behind. I saw, through the scope, the spray. He landed face-flat in the dirt.

I looked up. The only soldier aiming that way was Feldman. He had no scope—I hadn't issued him one yet—and he was squinting down the iron sights, trying to see his man.

The first thought that occurred to me was what a remarkable shot he was.

It took us until sundown, availing ourselves of close air support, to exfil home. There was no hope of recovering the kid, who in any case had been a goner before he'd hit the ground. As soon as we got back inside the wire, Private Dupree jumped

Feldman. He got in several vicious punches before anyone tried to pull him off. I sent Feldman to the aid station, where he stayed for the rest of the evening. Later, I brought him some food. He was sitting on the floor, holding a cold pack to his swollen brow. After muttering some bromides about collateral damage, the nature of combat, I said, "Don't worry about the report."

For a moment I thought Feldman was going to object; to insist on suffering some consequences for his actions; to say, "I killed that child, and I need to pay." I could see the noble temptation flickering like a loose bulb behind his eyes.

Then it went out.

I DIDN'T REALLY talk to Feldman for several weeks after that. None of us did. If before he'd been a minor nuisance, unfortunate but innocuous enough, now the old man was a bona fide pariah. McPherson no longer put forth the effort to find excuses to rebuke or punish him, and the rest of the platoon, understanding this to be a still harsher form of rebuke and punishment, followed suit. Feldman was considerate. He made avoiding him as easy as he could.

A month or so after the ambush at the creek, I received word that the chaplain was making the rounds and would be at the patrol base in the morning. That night I waited until Murray hit the shower, and I called Feldman into the box.

His appearance disturbed me. What little hair he had was way too long—far exceeding regulation. It made him look even older, more incongruous in that place, and less like a soldier. I could only imagine what McPherson, in the past, would have done to him. Now, it seemed, no one had noticed.

I said, "I was thinking it might be a good idea for you to talk to someone, Feldman."

There was evident relief in his eyes. Evident gratitude. "I appreciate that, sir," he said.

"Good. So you agree."

Feldman vigorously nodded. "If you want to know the truth, sir, the truth is that if it weren't for my kids, I might just go ahead and . . ." He laughed. "But then, I can't even *think* about my kids without thinking about . . ."

I cleared my throat. "What I was going to say is the chaplain will be here tomorrow, and he'd probably be a good person to talk to."

Feldman blinked.

"Better than me, probably," I added.

He had the same stupid, befuddled look on his face as when he'd thought that McPherson really wanted to hear about the book he was reading.

"I'm sorry, sir."

"They're trained in this stuff," I said. I picked up a stack of papers from the table and began flipping through them, stopping occasionally to set one facedown on a different stack.

"Should I go now?" Feldman asked.

I glanced up as if surprised to find him still standing there. "Sure, Feldman," I said. "And do me a favor, will you? Cut your fucking hair."

The next morning Corporal Sanchez was the only soldier at mass, and Feldman steered clear of the chaplain for the rest of the day. It was only much later that I learned that Feldman was a Jewish name—although, by then, I knew that no priest, rabbi, or other person could have helped him anyway.

OURS WAS A WAR that offered few opportunities, aside from getting killed or wounded, to distinguish yourself. There were no hills to charge, peninsulas to hold, bridges to seize. There was only the patrol: a year's worth of mine-littered walks ending where they started. Maybe this is why it was with a kind of horny impatience that we kept waiting for the big one, some mad battle in retribution for Feldman's crime.

As usual, when it came it was a letdown.

We were finally returning to the compound by the river, which we'd postponed doing since the ambush. We'd made it past the grove and the creek bed, the chaparral where the kid had died. We were almost there, about a dozen meters from the property, when a slot in the metal gate slid open, a muzzle poked out, and someone from inside opened fire.

It lasted maybe five seconds. Neither of the two shots came anywhere near us. The gate was flimsy tin, and before the gunman could get off a third round we'd riddled it with holes. We fanned out and readied for the others. Incredibly, there were none.

"The hell?" McPherson said.

Bruce and Sanchez opened the gate. As they swung it wide, we all braced in anticipation, weapons raised. What they revealed was a shot-up corpse slumped in a wheelchair. The man had taken several bullets in the face; it was difficult to judge his age. Both of his feet were missing. Not his legs—just his feet. A Kalashnikov lay across his lap.

Sanchez patted him down. He shrugged.

"The hell?" McPherson said.

Once again, we found nothing suspicious in the compound. There were only a few mud rooms, cell-like, each with a narrow entrance obstructed by a tacked-up sheet. The sheets were floral-patterned.

I peeked into each of the rooms after they'd been cleared. All but one held farm equipment, engine parts, hay, and chickens.

The sole space dedicated to human living was crammed with bedding and pillows. Colorful tapestries hung from the walls. A wooden chest stood in a corner. The soldiers had yanked out all the drawers: clothes lay in messy piles atop the cushions and blankets. I noticed that some were the clothes of a child. I sifted through them with my boot. Did I know what I was looking for? Was I surprised when I found the brown prayer cap, the *kameez* with the familiar pattern stitched across its chest in white and gold?

Sanchez was calling me on the radio: "You better come and see this, sir."

I joined him behind the compound, where we'd neglected to search during the night-op, under the shade of a pomegranate tree. He stood at the lip of a yawning hole in the ground. The hole looked like the mouth of a small volcano, sloping gently, and then vertically, into a pit of uncertain depth. It was a karez: part of a labyrinth of subterranean passageways built millennia ago to transport water from desert aquifers. The system had long since dried up, leaving beneath the village a complex network of tunnels, some big enough to drive a truck through. These tunnels obsessed the CO, who was convinced that the enemy used them to travel from village to village, stash matériel, and convene *shuras* undetected by the drones. He'd once confided in me that he wouldn't be surprised if there was a whole "Taliban city" down there, complete with power and roads. Of course, the implied image was the CO descending with a flame-thrower, hordes of screaming gooks running out on fire. Like I say, though, ours was a lackluster war: rarely did it yield such lurid satisfactions. We'd searched dozens of these caverns, and not once had we ever found anything.

Sanchez turned on his flashlight.

"Merry Christmas," he said.

What we discovered, after Bruce rappelled to the bottom, was a burlap sack containing almost two hundred pounds of ammonium nitrate, some blasting caps, and a couple dozen carbon rods. No Taliban city, exactly, but a haul.

I FOUND SPECIALIST Feldman pulling security near the gate, brought him to the wheelchair, and made him look.

I explained how this fucking hajji—who'd attacked us, who'd been hiding enough shit to blow up half the village, who'd lost his own feet during some mishap in the workshop, and who, for all we knew, had been responsible for Kahananui and the others—this fucking hajji was the father of the kid. "Or grandfather," I said. "Or brother. Point is, the kid lived here. They lived here together."

Before I'd even finished I regretted it. Feldman gazed down at that brutalized corpse, and I could see him working it out. He was smart, after all, in his way. Too smart for the infantry, anyhow—although, fatally, not smart enough to have seen that in the first place. Just as I'd told Feldman one story, another was telling itself. I mean the story in which the kid was exactly who we'd wanted him to be; the story in which he'd tried to help us with the bombs because it had been a bomb that maimed his father, grandfather, brother, or whoever; the story in which the kid had followed us not just that day of the ambush at the creek but every day, ever since we'd arrived in the village and erected the patrol base; the story in which he saw for himself what happened to Kahananui, and he pitied us; the story in which this footless, faceless person had volunteered the use of his karez and launched his pathetic little kamikaze raid only after we had killed the kid; and the story in which Specialist Feldman, far from forestalling a catastrophe, as I'd suggested, was in a sense responsible for two deaths now, not one.

This story was as plausible as mine, mine as plausible as this one, and who could say how many other variations there might be, or which of them Feldman was contemplating then.

It didn't matter. He had the rest of his shitty life to attend to all of them. The rest of his shitty life: and still he'd get no closer to knowing. No closer than Sergeant Walsh will get to knowing whether that boy in Baghdad set him up or warned him. No closer than I will get to knowing whether the weight of that radio was the weight that killed Kahananui.

ONE DAY, TOWARD the end of our deployment, Murray told me he had something he wanted to show me. He reached into the gym bag he kept under the monitor and brought out an unopened can of Dr Pepper. It was the first Dr Pepper I'd seen since my leave, nine months ago. He'd been squirrelling it all this time.

"It's going in my first machine," Murray said. Then he went on to explain how he intended to use the money he'd earned in Afghanistan to invest in the "pop-vending racket." "There's only one word you need to know to make your fortune," said Murray, "and I'm about to tell you what it is." He tossed me the Dr Pepper can, and I held it in my palm, feeling its heft, its promise. "Location," Murray said.

Back at Knox, I pinned the new ribbons on my dress blues, spoke at the memorials, completed my contract, and took the discharge. I saw the old platoon once more, about six months later, at a bar in Louisville. McPherson had organized a party to celebrate Sanchez getting his citizenship. When I arrived,

Sanchez was parading around in a cardboard Uncle Sam hat. I'd been apprehensive about seeing McPherson, but as soon as I walked in, he threw his arm on me, yelled for everyone's attention, and proposed a toast. He called me the best lieutenant he'd ever had the privilege to serve under, and all of the men duly agreed.

I sat in a booth with Rob Dupree. He was a corporal now, a budding McPherson. You could see the sergeant's influence on him. He told me they'd already been put on alert again, and he seemed pleased. A little later, he said, "Look who it is."

I turned to find Feldman stepping through the door. He wore a plaid shirt tucked into pleated slacks. He still looked like a math teacher.

"How's he been doing?" I said.

Dupree shrugged. Then he told me something strange. He told me that Feldman had re-upped, extending his contract for another four years.

"He's not so bad," said Dupree.

I watched Feldman navigate the crowd. I could see that things had improved for him. No one turned his back or snubbed him; no one called him "Sorry." Still, after a few polite greetings, silent nods, Feldman was at the bar, on a stool, by himself.

Eventually, I headed that way. Just before I reached him, I glimpsed Feldman's face in the mirror above the taps. It stopped me cold. I was standing there, a foot or two behind Feldman, when someone yelled "Sir!" and I seized the chance to turn around, away from him, into the middle of a war story. It was a familiar one, a story we'd all heard and told a dozen times but that we still laughed and shook our heads at, even though it wasn't true.

THE PORT IS NEAR

THE SUN IS LOW ON THE HEADLANDS AND THE WHOLE empty bay alive with slippery light. On my way down the ramp I stop to admire the fleet. Not even a dozen bow-pickers remain. They are all listing and jury-rigged: plastic duct-taped over broken windows, rotten plywood bolted to aluminum. What with the salvaged tires hanging from the rails, the Styrofoam coolers bungee-corded to the cabin roofs, the impression you have is of a rogue armada of waterborne jalopies. On the deck of the *Captain Smilie*, Bud Jr. attends to a mini camping grill with a set of tongs. When I pass him on the dock, he eyeballs the flare gun in my hand.

"Fixing to sink?" he asks.

Before I can explain, Bud Sr. emerges from the cabin carrying a Tupperware container full of brown sauce.

"Make way," he tells Bud Jr.

"Let me turn 'em," Bud Jr. says.

"Give 'em a minute," says Bud Sr.

"In a minute they'll be burnt."

"Hear that?" Bud Sr. asks me.

"Like yours burnt?" Bud Jr. asks me.

"I work for Sal," I say, meaning barbecue particulars are not often my concern.

Bud Sr. removes his gimme cap and itches his bald head with the edge of its bill. "I don't know how you do it," he says.

"Do what?"

"Stand that ornery dago."

When I reach the *Lady Barbara*, I find that Sal is out again, slumped on a bucket turned into a stool. Across his lap, the damaged net; in his fists, the shuttle and twine. A monument to dotage, complete with bird turds. All around him, gulls flock and shit.

I climb aboard. Inside the cabin, while stowing the gun, I hear a sputter from below. I roll back the carpet, open the hatch, wiggle down. The pump is clogged: foul, dark water stands in the bilge. I disassemble the housing—there, jammed in the filter, is Sal's lucky handkerchief. At first I delight in the prospect of how I will gloat. Then I realize: he's been down here tinkering again. Someday, I swear, I will find that geezer wrapped on the propeller shaft.

When I return to the deck, Sal is wide awake, weaving the shuttle through the web, humming a ditty. "Said, 'Get flares,'" he tells me, "not, 'Fuck off for the afternoon.'"

"I been back an hour," I say.

"Bet you can screw an hour too," says Sal.

He holds up the net for me to see. Last night, on the flats off Sausalito, we snagged a boulder. The gash it made was big enough to step through. "Unmendable," I declared. Now I wish I hadn't. Somehow, Sal has restored the ravaged mesh to a near-perfect grid: the diamonds all proportionate, the knots small and tight.

"Mendable," he says.

I change the subject. "The Buds are barbecuing."

Sal shows no response. It happens more and more, that. Each time, I am less sure he's just ignoring me.

"The Buds are barbecuing!" I shout.

"Christ. I'm right here."

"We're invited."

Sal harrumphs. "I'm doing mac and gravy."

On the *Barbara*, almost every night is mac-and-gravy night. Sal acts as if his is a secret family recipe, preserved from the Old Country. In fact, the macaroni is regular Barilla pasta, the gravy a liquidy blend of canned tomatoes, garlic, sugar.

"A pinch of sugar," Sal has said on more than one occasion. "That's what you're tasting."

My first season, when I made the mistake of tossing the tomato can after emptying it into the pot, Sal found it in the trash, filled it with water, and held it out for me to see. Inside was pinkish fluid.

"Gravy," Sal said.

After we eat, I haul up a gallon of bay water and wash the dishes. Suddenly, it's time. Sal starts the engine, I unwrap the breast lines, and we idle from the slip. A few tourists, having strayed from the attractions of Fisherman's Wharf, take pictures from the pier. Soon we are beyond the seawall and can feel the wind.

I MET SAL shortly after I returned to San Francisco. I say return. I'm not from there. I'd only lived there briefly, with a girl who was, before they attacked us and I volunteered. (I say they attacked us and I volunteered. The one didn't cause the other.) Still, when I got out, although the girl had moved to a different city, with a different fool, I could not come up with any better place to go.

I'd been unemployed for months, taking a lot of walks, when I wandered onto the unmarked turnoff at the end of Hyde Street. The only boat in harbor was the *Barbara*. I could hear Sal bellowing all the way from the ramp.

Eventually, a man stormed out of the cabin with a backpack on his shoulder, snatched a pair of slickers from the hooks, and disembarked. Sal was close behind. All I could make out was his cotton undershirt and red suspenders. As the man huffed away, Sal yelled at him in Italian. He brought his hands to his mouth, making a megaphone. "Shoemaker!" Sal cried.

The man neither looked back nor slowed down, just raised his arm and gave Sal the bird.

I passed him on the dock. When I got to the *Barbara*, I discovered that Sal was corpulent and geriatric. The suspenders were patterned with blue anchors and the undershirt with stains both work- and lunch-related. Before I could introduce myself, he said, "If you're here for the fucking harbor fee, tell Curtis I'll pay him next week."

"I don't know Curtis," I said.

Sal peered at me. "You a Marelli?"

"No, sir."

"What do you want, then?"

"A job."

Sal stepped to the rail to better see. "Ever decked a bow-picker?"

"No, sir."

"Drift-netter?"

"No, sir."

"Trawler? Dredger? Seiner? Any kind of boat? Any damn thing that floats?"

I shook my head.

Sal nodded. "You do the drugs?"

"No, sir."

"And you're sure you ain't a Marelli."

"What's a Marelli?"

"What's a Marelli!" Sal bayed. He slapped the rail and

hooted. Then he said it a second time—"What *is* a Marelli?"—
and welcomed me aboard.

THE EBB WANTS to take us out to sea. We buck it the other way,
along the Embarcadero, past the loading docks and the point.
When we reach McCovey Cove, in the shadow of the ballpark,
Sal says, "You're wondering why I made you buy them flares."

The clouds have lifted. He is steering from the deck and I
am on my knees, fixing tangled harnesses, unfucking a cluster.
There is something in his voice—it gives me a bad feeling. Before Sal can tell me what it is, we spot the Pedrotti crew, laying
out their gear along the hull of a moored tanker. Dominic Pedrotti reverses off the buoy, while his two sons, Lenny and Vito,
guide the corks and leads off the reel, over the roller, into the
drink. When they wind it back the net is empty.

"Barren grounds!" Sal shouts at the Pedrottis. "Last time
they put roe here I still had a working pecker!"

Big Dom is a humorless man. He has debts, a pretty wife.
As he motors by, he glowers darkly and says, "This whole bay is
barren, Sal."

It is true. How many times have I heard how the herring
used to spawn? How the milt would get so thick the anchors almost floated? Glory days, over long before I showed. Sal blames
the sea lions, and the city for protecting them. (Of course, gill-
ing every fish from Islais Creek to Tiburon, decade after decade,
had nothing to do with it.) Every profit-minded captain has
vamoosed—north to Bellingham or south to Monterey. Nowa-
days, only the families remain: fathers with nothing else to give
their sons, sons with no one else to be except their fathers. Per
custom, my take of almost zero gross is zero. But room and
board are free: a bunk like a coffin, daily mac and gravy.

It suits me. I am used to worse.

After a few skunk sets near Treasure Island, we ride the ebb back to the marina. It is while we are drifting on a slack tide, keyed into my kind of quiet, that Sal brings up the flares again. He sits in the captain's chair, gazing through the windshield. Across North Beach, Chinatown, Russian Hill, the lamps are yellow.

"Well?" he asks.

"Well what?"

"How about it?"

I look at the city. I am speechless.

Sal swivels the chair to face me squarely. "How much do you think Paulie got for the *Beaut*?" he says, meaning Paul Aparo, who, after failing to find a buyer last year, had to bring the *Western Beauty* to the wrecker, break her into pieces, and sell the pieces off for scrap.

"You're talking insurance fraud," I say.

Sal makes a face and bats away the quibble like it smells funky.

He is right. I don't know why I said it. Insurance fraud? That's not what bothers me.

ACCORDING TO THE BUDS, Sal went through deckhands, before me, at an approximate rate of two per season. Bud Jr. claims he's seen him reduce more than one salty dog to tears—among them two of the Marelli brothers. One weekend when the fishery was closed, says Junior, Jack Marelli asked why they alone were on the water, tracking shoals they couldn't catch. "Would you rather go to shore?" inquired Sal. When Jack responded yes, that's exactly what he rathered, Sal dropped him off on Alcatraz, where he had to camp out on the ramparts until the Monday-morning ferry could bring him back to San Francisco. When I asked Bud Jr. how Sal had managed, physically, to get Jack off the boat, Bud laughed and said, "Guy jumped."

None of the old-timers expected me to last the winter. Even now, they are unsure what to make of it. I can tell by the way they look at us: Bud Sr., Big Dom, and the rest. Don't ask me why. Sal and I have always tolerated each other. Maybe it's because, un-like Jack Marelli, I have never asked to come to shore—because, like Sal, there's no place there I have to be.

WE DON'T SPEAK of it again until the tide turns and the flood starts to tug us south.

Then I say, "I'll make you a deal."

Sal arches an eyebrow—a perfect chevron. On the one hand, he has already made up his mind and does not require my approval; on the other, he is an inveterate gambler.

"If we get a quarter-ton tonight," I say, "you don't go through with it. You finish the season. You put the boat on blocks."

"And if we're short?"

"I will cooperate with your harebrained gambit."

Sal throws back his head. He kneads his turkey neck with the air of a philosopher stroking his beard. "Three-quarters."

"No."

"Three-quarters or no deal."

"Sal."

"Up to you."

I sigh. "Half-ton."

"Half-ton?"

"But," I say, "I get to pick the sets."

Sal grins and extends his hand. "Even if I avoided them on purpose, I'd stand a better chance at half a ton than you."

"Not tonight," I say.

For a moment, when he sees the handkerchief pinched between my thumb and finger, black with leaked oil and hydraulic fluid, Sal is, for once, bamboozled. Then he swivels to the wheel, puts the boat in gear, and says, "Where to?"

WE HEAD EAST, across the tide, and can soon make out the shipyards of Richmond: loading cranes, like enormous steel animals, menacing the shore. I see color on the sonar and tell Sal to stop.

"That's plankton," he says.

"That's herring," I say.

We go out and pay a shackle or two of net into the water. Soon as they're wet Sal winds them back. I lean over the bow, watching the corks rise out of the black. Even several feet down I can see the iridescent bellies shimmering like coins as they are lifted from the deep. The first bunch drops like a sack onto the deck.

"Plankton?" I say.

Sal just sulks—but this time, I am sure he's heard. I find a plump female and break her open. Bright-orange roe spills like ripe fruit.

We clean the shackles, lay out the rest, throw the anchor. In the cabin, I light the stove while Sal folds down the table and deals the cards.

We are a couple games in when he says, "Whatever happens, this is my last season."

I focus on my hand; after a minute, Sal adds, "If you had any sense, it'd be yours too."

Later, while he shuffles, I catch him glancing at the sonar.

He goes to the stove, opens the carburetor, and lets more diesel onto the flame. "My way," he says when he sits down, "we get out with cash."

"Who said I'm getting out?"

Sal deals. For a time, he is silent. Then he says, "I'm not giving you the boat. Forget about that."

I laugh and shake my head like that is the last thing I would want. But I know that if I try to say so, my voice will fail me.

Sal, he knows too.

JUST BEFORE DAWN, we go out to have a look. The fog advances like a ghost glacier down the Carquinez, toward the Pacific. Sal controls the reel while I help the gear into the bow. When the first bunch plunks over, my stomach turns. A number of herring are gilled in the web; a third of them, though, are decapitated heads, no bodies. Another third are gutted bodies, no heads.

"Sea lions," I say.

Sal manages not to comment. Anyhow, even with most of the net picked clean, it is a haul. I rake them into the hole, and we both stand over that mess, reckoning.

It's close. It could be half a ton.

BETWEEN SEASONS, Sal always kept me busy. After the close, we'd take the boat up the Sacramento, to his place in Collinsville. When Sal grew up there, he once told me, trains still stopped in town to be unbuckled and conveyed across the delta via barge; the waterfront was overrun with immigrants; Sal's father and uncles still harvested Chinook with the same wood-hulled feluccas they had sailed in Italy. By the time I saw it, Collinsville was a wind farm: pastures and turbines, the boarded-up homes of an entire county that had long since crossed the river to Contra Costa.

Sal's place stood on stilts, so close to the bank that during a big tide you could spit out the kitchen window into the water. A crooked dock extended from the front door, over the cattails, all the way to where the bottom dropped. When I wasn't working on the *Barbara*, or performing renovations on Sal's house, barn, yard, skiffs, and vehicles, I'd swim for hours in that brackish current—lie for hours on those weathered, sunbaked planks.

Sal napped most of the day. In the evenings, he'd come out with a case of Michelob, a can of night crawlers, and we would seat a couple rods in the flag holders he'd screwed into the pilings. The Chinook were long gone, but you could still get a sturgeon. If it was a monster, Sal would tie a line around its tail and keep it leashed there in the shallows.

Once or twice, after a few beers, I was able to coax out of him a reminiscence or two about the war. What he survived in Korea was so much worse than anything I ever had to deal with, it seems unfair to call it by the same name. Still, I often talked about Afghanistan—because I wanted to, for one, and because I thought it might inspire Sal to do the same. Usually it didn't. I remember one night, watching the suburban glow bloom over Contra Costa, I started telling him about the mosque. I'd never told anybody about the mosque. If I couldn't entertain him, I guess I figured, I would at least appall the man. Before I got very far, Sal pushed himself up from his lawn chair, staggered to the end of the dock, and pissed.

"The only thing these stories are good for is getting laid," he said. "And I'm not fucking you."

———

WHEN WE ARRIVE at the pump, most of the fleet is already in line. The Pedrottis are up front—Big Dom on the pier, talking to the buyer. The buyer wears a suit and tie, galoshes, and a hooded windbreaker. He holds a storage clipboard, the kind that opens, stacked with carbon-copy receipts. He is the last buyer of herring left in San Francisco, and he knows it. As usual, he is telling Dominic something Dominic does not want to hear. They both look at the scale, not each other.

When it's our turn, I tie the *Barbara* to the pilings and Sal steps onto the gunwale. He waits for a swell to lift him nearer the ladder. Beneath the pier, row after row of panes of sun angle down from between the planks. They make electric lines that squiggle on the moving water. Pigeons pace the joists, drop from their perches, flash through the panes.

Up top, several captains watch Sal with concern. When Sal reaches them, the buyer hooks him under the arm and helps him up.

"Waitin' for that fuckin' thing to fall off?" Sal says.

The pump operator swings out a big hose suspended from a metal boom; I open the hatch and guide it into the hole. The operator presses a button, and the pump bucks to life.

"That it?" he asks after a minute.

"Hold on."

I climb into the hole. A few fish remain—on the sides, in the corners. I suction them up.

Ten minutes or more go by before Sal reappears at the top of the ladder. In his hand he holds the receipt.

I do not need to see it.

I can tell by the look on his face.

———

THE MOOD AT the harbor is more upbeat than usual. Most of the crews made market, and the fog has lifted to reveal, of all things, the sun. While Sal sleeps, I visit the *Captain Smilie*. Both Buds are supine on the deck, shirts off and draped across their faces. Bud Sr. glistens with tanning oil, his chest hair gooped and matted like a buildup in a drain. "That better be a cloud," he says when my shadow lands on him.

"I come humbly, in search of wisdom," I say.

Bud Sr. holds up a finger while the broadcaster on his portable radio narrates a play. Then he gropes for the dial and turns the volume down. He rolls the finger, inviting me to speak.

"Who's Barbara?" I say.

It is a question I have never asked. Shy as he is on Korea, Sal has even less to say about his family. It was the Buds who told me "the diabetes" killed his wife, and it was from them that I learned about his son. Rumors on the fallout abound. During my time in Collinsville, I have never seen him.

Bud Sr. clasps his hands behind his head, exposing the pale sides of his arms. "Barbara as in the *Lady Barbara*?" he says.

"No," says Bud Jr. "As in Barbara Walters. As in Barbara Bush. As in—"

Quick as a diving pelican, Bud Sr. snatches the shirt from Bud Jr.'s face and flings it over the rail.

"Really?" says Bud Jr. Then he gets up to go find the gaff hook.

"Yes," I say, "as in the *Lady Barbara*."

"Barbara was Mario's mother," Bud Sr. says.

"Who's Mario?"

"Mario Apuzzo."

I wait for Bud Sr. to elaborate. When, instead, he turns the volume back up on the radio, I say, "This Mario. Sal had something with his mother?"

Bud Sr. sits up on his elbows. His face looks like he just smashed his hand or touched something hot. "You're another one, aren't you?" he says. "No wonder you and Sal get on."

"Sal didn't have something with his mother?"

"Sal bought the boat from Mario," Bud Sr. says. "Just never changed the name."

WHEN I RETURN to the *Barbara*, Sal is sitting at the table, a cardboard box before him. The box contains some rubber-banded paperwork and other miscellany: the wood fid his father used for splicing lines, his dog tags from Korea, a piece of whalebone with a ship scrimshawed on it. I am to take the box, along with whatever belongings of my own I don't wish to contribute to Davy Jones's locker, to Sal's truck on Hyde Street. Then I am to drive to Collinsville. Later, while Sal plays senile, I will tell whatever investigators the insurance company dispatches that I went to Sal's to collect a new net. It's a decent plan. Half the fleet saw us snag that boulder on the flats off Sausalito.

I pack my bag and take up the box.

"This way, we get paid," Sal says.

On my trip up the ramp, no one looks twice. The box, the bag—both of them together might be a week's worth of trash.

OF COURSE, NO, it is not about getting paid. For some time now, he has been trying to drop me on the shore. There was the roofer, the sheetrocker, the painter, the plumber—all friends or relatives of Sal's. The job at which I lasted longest was as a laborer for a contractor. After a month, Rich Caruso put me with the carpenters, and by winter I was wearing a tool belt and running the saws. That year, when I showed up at the harbor a week before the season opened, Sal tried hard to look disappointed. Then he mumbled something in Italian, went inside, and returned with the mop.

"So now I have to hear it from Richie too?" he said.

I DON'T DRIVE to Collinsville. I sit in Sal's truck on the wharf until the sun goes down, and then I sneak back to the harbor. Nothing moves in the cabin of the *Barbara*; no doubt Sal is dozing. I get aboard as quietly as possible, and, as quietly as possible, I open the hatch and ease into the hole.

I have to crouch there, in two inches of bloody water, for nearly an hour before the engine rumbles on. When we pass the seawall, Sal turns west, toward the Golden Gate. Soon the hull lifts and slaps in the rough confluence where the breakers meet the bay. The engine dies, and I climb onto the deck.

The bridge is not very far behind us, its towers red in the upturned lamps. Still, almost right away, I can feel it: how hard the ebb is ripping—the profound tow of all those rivers, deltas, estuaries forcing through the narrow gap between the headlands and Fort Point.

The bridge recedes. Within minutes we are carried past Bonita Cove, the lighthouse, into the Pacific. I go inside to tell Sal to head back toward the mouth. The carpet is rolled up, the floor hatch to the engine room propped open. Sal squats down there with a penlight in his teeth, already wearing his orange survival suit. I catch him just as he is fitting an Allen wrench into the drainage plug's hexagonal groove.

"Sal," I say.

He looks up, shining the light in my face. I am about to tell him to hold on, wait a second, when he torques the wrench and a jet of water blasts the plug out of the floor.

IT TAKES A while for the engine room to flood. Sal won't talk to me. (All he says is, "Aren't you supposed to be in Collinsville?") When the sea bubbles like a spring into the cabin, he radios the Coast Guard. By then, the bridge is just a pulsing tendril about to snap somewhere between San Francisco and Marin. The lighthouse blinks, but we are well beyond the reach of its beam. I follow Sal to the deck. Eventually, like that, the cabin lurches under, pulling the bow down behind it. Then we are floating.

"Stay close," Sal says.

The suits keep us buoyant and dry and not quite freezing. The tide, though, is irresistible, and soon I lose sight of Sal. I look around. A faint bonfire smolders on Baker Beach. I yell Sal's name, but he doesn't answer. I yell louder. There is only the static of the surf on the rocks.

At some point a flare drags a bright tail into the night. It describes a steep arc and at its zenith bursts into a rain of electric color. For a few moments, it lights everything.

A HUMAN CRY

THEY WERE DOGGING BEAR AGAIN. IT WAS THE THIRD night in as many weeks he'd been woken by the bawling hounds. Tom Mayeaux listened, wishing them to turn. When they didn't—when, instead, there came the unmistakable din of the pack baying their quarry down the ridge, straight onto Tucker land—he got up, pulled on his boots, and lumbered from the bed-and-toilet end of his Airstream to the dinette-and-stove end. The .30-.30 leaned beside the door. Mayeaux slung it on his shoulder and stepped into the rain.

He'd left the flatbed window down. The seat's non-upholstered foam, absorbent as a sponge, emptied when he sat on it. By the time he reached the wetlands, it looked like he had pissed himself. Mayeaux turned off the engine and could hear, away up on the dark ridge, the four-wheelers revving on the fire road, the dogs that they pursued lining out for Gypsum Creek. He walked into the trees.

For a while, the canopy did not admit the rain. But soon that tightly knitted weft thinned to open sky. The ground began to squish. Back when Nate Tucker first hired Mayeaux to help out with the hogs, this clearing had been a meadow, all deer brush and pussy tow. Now it was marsh. If the beavers kept it up, they'd soon have themselves a lake. Used to be, Nate and Tom would wade out in the cattails, snipe those bastards all day long. That—beaver culling—was another thing Hannah put an end to.

The hounds had splashed through the mud and sedge to an elevated hummock, where they surrounded a skinny pine, snapping teeth and yowling. Up in the tree, the spooked black bear hugged trunk. Mayeaux found some cover downwind in the grass. He eased into the prone and drew a bead on what seemed to him the lead dog: a slobbering Plott in a thick steel choke collar. He waited, getting rained on.

When at last the poachers caught up, the weather had moved; a break in the clouds allowed some starlight on the scene. Sure enough, it was Dave Campbell and Leo DeMint.

Mayeaux watched them slosh up to the dogs. DeMint produced a Magnum from his belt and held it on the bruin while Campbell dragged the hounds one at a time to the far slope of the hummock. When he returned from tying up the last of the pack, the two men stood together, considering their game. It was not much of a trophy, still just a yearling—ears laid back in terror, hackles sunk like nails in the rough bark of the pine. Nonetheless, DeMint steadied the Mag and put a bullet through its skull. The bruin tumbled down, snapping brittle branches, landing with a thud. Leo rolled it over and Dave brought out from his ruck the block and tackle.

THE NEXT MORNING he woke to an angry fist hammering the Airstream. It was Saturday. If Hannah wanted to forgo the courtesy of waiting until the afternoon to upbraid him, Mayeaux would forgo the courtesy of putting on his pants. He was about to open the door, the remnants of an a.m. chubby still nudging at his skivvies, when he recalled his teeth, lunged back to the bed-and-toilet end, plucked them dripping from the mason jar, and jammed them in his mouth.

Hannah Tucker stood beside the flatbed.

"Barn on fire?" asked Mayeaux.

"Are you going to stand there and tell me you didn't hear it?" Hannah said.

She was old enough to be his mother. All the same: that figure. Today it was concealed under an oversize sweater. When she gathered up her graying hair to snap a rubber band from her wrist onto a ponytail, she had first to raise her hand and let the baggy sleeve slink down. Mayeaux's near nakedness hadn't fazed her in the least.

"Heard what?" he said.

Hannah put her foot on the bumper of the flatbed. The way she did it seemed intended to remind him whose it was.

"Hounds? A gunshot? But let me guess: you slept through that too."

Mayeaux sat down in the doorway, looking at his dirty socks. His mouth felt full. He jiggled the top dentures with his thumb. Suddenly, he missed his pants.

"Negligent discharge, probably," he said. "You know these bear guys. They're just out to grabass, exercise the pups, more than really hunt."

"They can grabass all they want. Grabass, circle jerk, hump the pups. They can hump each other—on someone else's land." Hannah shook her head. "It's no hunter needs to tree his game."

"Not much sport in it," Tom agreed.

"That shot was near the wetlands. If they got one, maybe they field dressed it. Why don't you go have a look? See if you can find some guts."

"Sure, Hannah."

"Before the critters get to it."

"I'll go today."

Hannah nodded and turned to head back toward the house.

"First, though," Mayeaux called after her, "I thought we

could discuss the hogs." He knew it was bad timing. But with Hannah, there was no good time when it came to talking hogs.

She kept walking. "Just see if you can find some guts."

THE TUCKER HOUSE stood at the top of a wide grassy slope. At the bottom of the slope, shaded by a line of aspen, stood the disused barn and sty. The sty consisted of a cement-floored pig hutch, with steel pipe partitions, and an outdoor pen. There, an old boar and two sows still liked to root and wallow. Mayeaux shoveled the bear organs from a wheelbarrow to the slop trough. He watched them come and get it. The windpipe and gullet, the genitals, anus, heart, and lungs—them hogs snarfed up the whole fly-swarmed anatomy like it was theirs, they needed it back.

God, Tom loved them. Year after year, with a couple others, they'd farrowed two healthy litters each. That was sixty-something shoats to fatten, butcher, and string up in the smokehouse with hickory and beech. A profitable operation—until Nate died and Hannah decided it felt "wrong" to keep it going. A week after the funeral, she'd told Mayeaux to slaughter all their breeding stock: she was finished raising hogs. Appalled, Mayeaux had waited until Hannah came down to the sty, then staved in the first sow's head with the blunt end of a poleax. Just brained her.

"Jesus!" Hannah had cried, and before she could exclaim again Mayeaux'd killed in identical fashion the next one in line.

That did. She let him keep the others.

After inhaling the bruin innards, the boar shit all over. Mayeaux took the shovel. It was a pity, wasting such high-grade manure on the grass.

"Good as it stinks," Nate Tucker used to say.

They had sold it by the truckload to half the farms in Plumas.

HE WAS ON the tractor, turning up the slope from the barn, when Hannah got back from town. She idled the Suburban, rolled down her window, and yelled. Mayeaux pulled alongside her, pointing at his ear.

"What are you doing?" Hannah repeated.

"Mowing."

"Did you have a look?"

Mayeaux nodded.

"And?"

"All I seen was beavers."

Unamused, Hannah told him, "I went to the sheriff's. I talked to Henry Parson."

"Did, did you?"

"He said he'd ask around."

Mayeaux leaned over on the tractor seat and spat. "Surprised he didn't want to dust the woods for prints."

Henry was no friend of his. The day of the accident, then–Deputy Parson had driven out to the property and asked Mayeaux to show him exactly where he'd been when Nate got tangled up. He'd crossed the muddy pen himself and stood inside the hutch, squinting through the door.

"Say you couldn't see him?" he'd asked, pointing at the bloodied mower. When Mayeaux explained that the door had not been open, Henry actually grabbed the loop of bailing wire that functioned as its latch and pulled it shut. There'd ensued some awkward seconds, then, as the door creaked back on its own. Henry, as if he'd just sleuthed out the smoking gun, made a show of studying the unplumb hinges until Tom said, "You have to hook this one, Deputy," and closed it again, this time catching the wire on a bent nail that protruded from the jamb.

Henry Parson nodded. "You were in the service, is that what I heard?"

"Yes."

"What branch?"

"Army."

"I was in the service," Henry said. "Air force. It was peacetime. I was in logistics."

To this, Mayeaux could not think of anything to say.

Henry shrugged. "Anyway. You used to run around with Dave Campbell?"

"I ain't seen Dave for a while."

"Ain't you?" Henry said, and Mayeaux was unsure whether he was consciously mocking his accent or unconsciously echoing it. "Where you from?" Henry asked. "Originally, I mean."

Mayeaux told him. The deputy nodded as if it confirmed some niggling suspicion of his. He unlatched the door and gazed out at the tractor again.

"Goddamn tragedy," he said.

"Yes, it is," said Mayeaux.

DAVE CAMPBELL CALLED what he lived in a mobile home. If you wanted to ruffle Dave's feathers, you called it a trailer. Mayeaux and Campbell had disagreed on this point many, many times. Usually, Campbell's argument hewed to specs. His rig measured nearly seventy feet—twice the length of Mayeaux's Airstream. Plus it had no wheels. Plus double-pane windows on all four sides.

Mayeaux's response: Didn't one side have a hitch?

He parked down the road and snuck around the back. A garden hose snaked past chain-link kennels and tarp-covered quads. Mayeaux followed it. The hose led to a steel tub covered with a sheet of plywood. Inside the tub, fascia scraped to silky hide, the young bear's pelt in a bath of saltwater and alum.

A light flashed on. Behind him, someone told Mayeaux to put them up.

Mayeaux let down the plywood and raised his arms. He turned around. Dave Campbell had the Magnum trained on him.

Squinting at Mayeaux, Dave lowered the gun.

"Tommy?" he said.

IN THE DEN, Leo DeMint sat on the sofa and a big girl Mayeaux didn't recognize sat beside him, one fishnetted hock draped on his knee, little flesh diamonds pushing through the webbing like a string-tied ham. A second girl, in dirty white jeans and a Minnie Mouse sweatshirt, sat sideways in the La-Z-Boy. When Campbell rapped her feet, she groaned, got up, and let him take her spot. Then she fell onto his lap.

Dave Campbell wore a camouflage hat with a duct-taped buckle and a worn-out bill. His four blueticks lay on the carpet, staring up at Tom and panting. Campbell and DeMint, the girls—they all had the skin, the teeth, the nails, the eyes.

"Who is he?" asked the girl in the Minnie Mouse sweatshirt, Campbell's girl.

Campbell ignored her. "So, what, you're here to party?" he asked Mayeaux.

"If he is, I'm leaving," DeMint said. "You know how Tommy gets."

"How does he get?" asked Campbell's girl.

"Tell her, Tommy," said DeMint.

Mayeaux shook his head. "You need a new place to hunt," he said to Dave.

"I don't believe it," DeMint said. "She sent him here to set us straight."

"You already got one," Mayeaux said.

"That's Leo's," Campbell said.

"Yeah," said the girl on the couch, the big girl, Leo's girl. "That's Leo's."

"I don't like him," Campbell's girl said.

Dave cupped her jaw with one hand and squeezed, making fish lips. "Shhh," he said, and with his other hand pressed a finger to the lips.

"She went to the sheriff," Mayeaux said.

Campbell and DeMint exchanged a look.

"Henry?" Campbell said.

"Sure it weren't a social call?" DeMint said.

"Social," laughed Dave.

"Who's Henry?" asked the girl.

Campbell glared at her, no longer laughing. He shoved her to the floor.

"Fuck I do?" she said.

"Just keep off her place," said Mayeaux.

"Or what?" said DeMint.

"Yeah, or what?" said DeMint's girl.

Campbell yawned. "Everybody relax."

"We're not the ones who need to relax," the girl on the floor said. "Don't tell us to relax."

Mayeaux made to leave. Before he got very far, DeMint called to him. "What's it you do up there, anyway, now you don't got no hogs to stick?"

The big girl chortled.

"Looks like you're the hog sticker," Mayeaux said on his way out.

———

ONE EVENING IN November the sky turned green instead of gray. A charged current rocked the Airstream on its blocks. Through the window, Mayeaux saw bats flopping through the raving air, then realized they were shingles peeling off the outhouse roof. He hustled to the flatbed and headed for Hannah's. An uprooted sapling lodged into the grille. It flipped onto the hood and continued down the drive—a rabid monster, many-legged and on the run.

A patrol car was parked next to the Suburban. Mayeaux reached the front door just as Henry Parson opened it.

He was not in uniform. He wore blue jeans and a flannel, wool socks, no shoes.

"Where's your slicker?" Henry said. He turned and hollered toward the kitchen: "Hannah! Tom's here! Got a towel or something for him?"

Mayeaux hadn't been inside since Nate died. He'd forgotten how much house it was. The high, slanted ceiling with its exposed cedar beams; the two-story window that looked onto the ridge. Flames popped in a gaping fieldstone fireplace. Henry held the poker in his hand.

Hannah came into the living room with two steaming mugs. She gave one to Henry, looked at Tom. "You're dripping on the floor," she said.

"Got a towel or something?" Henry said.

"I'm all right," said Mayeaux.

"Bull," Henry said. "Hannah, for Christ's sake, would you get the kid a towel?"

Mayeaux watched in amazement as Hannah went down the hall. He'd never seen her bossed like that.

Henry drifted to the fire. He lifted the tea bag from his mug and swung it by the string into the flames.

Mayeaux listened to it hiss. Soon as he'd entered he'd felt a difference in the room—something other than the sheriff. Now he realized: Nate's deer mounts were gone. He'd had half a dozen buck heads on the walls. Hannah had removed them.

"Glad I was able to help, by the way," Henry Parson said. "I want you to feel like you can always come to me for that sort of thing."

"What sort of thing?"

"Them poachers," Henry said.

"You got them?"

"*Got* them? No. I just sort of put the word out. It wasn't gonna stand."

"Uh-huh," said Mayeaux.

Henry stabbed the logs. He set his mug on the mantel, leaned the poker on the stones, and arranged himself into a model of reproof. "What's with the tone, son?" he said.

Mayeaux shrugged. "No tone."

Lightning flashed and for a moment the huge black window came to life with a lurid ghost country that smoldered for a while on the liquid pane.

Henry laughed. "What in the hell is that woman doing?"

"I'm going," said Mayeaux.

"In this? At least dry out first." Henry scowled and turned back toward the hall. "Hannah! Still waitin' on that towel!"

THE NEXT MORNING Mayeaux hiked into the woods, climbing over jacksawed pines, following the roar of flooded Gypsum Creek. At the wetlands, he found the dams in disarray, their mud-mortared logs scattered in the marsh. He passed a blasted redwood scarred by strips of blown-out bark, pale cambium and heartwood spilling from its ruined trunk. Eventually, he reached the sheltered glade where he and Campbell used to grow. The black hoses still lay in the weeds, old beer cans and broken bottles, the lawn chair Dave used to sit and smoke in. Roughly twenty plants they'd had—a good sixty pounds a run. Mayeaux crossed the glade. From where he stood, through the brush, he could see the barn, the slope, the house, the sty.

One afternoon, while checking on the irrigation, Mayeaux had heard what sounded like a human cry. Back in the trees, he'd found two animals wrangling on the ground. A fisher cat, it appeared, and a doe. Both were bloodied and plastered with wet leaves. Mayeaux grabbed a branch and brandished it. The fisher scurried off. For a long time, the doe wobbled on its stiltlike legs. Then it charged at Tom and jumped into his arms.

Mayeaux held it. He felt the doe's thin hide; beneath the hide, the ribs; beneath the ribs, the lungs; beneath the lungs, a warmth; beneath the warmth, a shudder. He recognized that shudder. It was a response to sounds he couldn't hear, odors he couldn't smell, and dangers of which he, Mayeaux, would never have to be afraid.

Later, when he told Nate about it, Nate snorted. "It's a fisher cat cries like that!" he said, and laughed at Tom for succoring the real killer after chasing off its victim with a stick.

A WEEK AFTER the storm, Hannah told Mayeaux that she would spend the next few months in Tahoe, with her sister. She didn't have it in her, she explained: a whole winter out there alone.

He helped her pack up the Suburban. Before she pulled away, Hannah rolled her window down. "About the pigs," she said.

"We can talk when you get back."

"I want it done while I'm gone."

"I hear you. But why decide right now?"

"I'm not," Hannah said.

He'd known it was coming. Even so, the following week, when he slaughtered and butchered the boar and sows, Mayeaux was unprepared for the loneliness that gripped him. The problem was that Leo had been right: although he did everything that needed to be done, and many things that didn't—although he mowed the field, painted the roof, stained the deck, cleaned the barn, chopped wood, cleared brush, and brought shit to the dump—without the hogs, there just was not enough to do.

He spent the next several weeks driving up and down the fire road, looking for trees felled during the storm. By December, he'd stacked enough split logs against the Airstream to keep it heated through half a dozen winters. It was around this time, they later reckoned, that he started visiting the house.

Hannah had left Mayeaux a key so that he could clear the pipes before they froze, and first he got into the habit of using her kitchen to prepare his lunch and supper. He built fires in the fireplace. He snooped around the rooms. Evenings, he sat at Nate's desk, in Nate's study, drinking Nate's booze. One night he stumbled to the closet where Hannah stored the deer mounts. Seizing a twelve-pointer by the antlers, he lugged it to the living room. The screws on which it once had hung still poked out from the wall. Mayeaux climbed onto a chair to catch them with the brackets. When he crashed, the impact popped his dentures clean out of his mouth.

Mayeaux scrambled after them. He fit them back onto his gums, went to the bathroom, checked the mirror. It looked like someone had hit him with a bat.

———

It was January when they came again. Earlier that afternoon the sun had broken out, melting the topmost layer of the snow and creating a liquidy slush that had since refrozen to form a brittle crust. As Mayeaux trudged toward the aspens, the .30-.30 on his shoulder and his jacket pocket full of ammo, his boots crunched through with every heavy step.

The hounds were down the ridge and square into the wetlands by the time he reached the creek. He stretched out on the far bank and loaded.

When the army had finally given him the dentures, Mayeaux had had to make an effort to try to smile more. Not until after he was discharged, went on the road, met the Tuckers, and settled in Plumas—where no one knew the teeth were fake—did he really find a knack for it. The day Nate died, Mayeaux had been practicing his smile while mowing the field. That was why he'd hit the stump.

Nate was in the hutch. When he heard the loud metallic clank, the blades slamming into wood, he came running out.

"Don't tell me," Nate said.

Mayeaux had his foot on the clutch. The engine idled; the drive shaft was engaged.

"Should I shut it down?"

Nate bent over the gear box, inspecting the bolts. "How many times?" he said. "How many times have you mowed this fuckin' field?"

"I'm gonna shut it down."

"If we need new blades," said Nate, "it's coming from your pay."

"That's fair."

"Is it? I guess you can afford it, can't you?" Then, yelling over the engine, Nate told Tom that he knew about the plants. He knew about Dave.

"What do you think she'll say when I tell her?" Nate asked. He shook his head. "I suggest you start thinking about where you're going next."

Those words! How those words would come to haunt Mayeaux!

Before he could think about it he'd done it. All he did was move his boot a smidge; the pedal leapt up on its own. When the shaft spun into action it snared a piece of Nate's clothing—the cuff of his jacket, maybe, or the tail of his shirt—and whipped him around several dozen times, each revolution pulping his face and legs against the steel blade carriage, the rocky ground. By the time Mayeaux reengaged the clutch, Nate was wrapped on the equipment like he was empty clothes. There were pieces of him everywhere; there was nothing but a gory rag.

A long time passed before Mayeaux turned around and looked. A long time he sat on that tractor, staring at those mountains in the pretty, pinkish light . . .

When the lead dog came thrashing out of the dark it didn't even slow, just kept flying full-bore into the shallows, straining its neck to breathe above the splash. Mayeaux nearly missed his chance, getting off a hurried round as the bluetick clambered at the bank. By dumb luck it was a head shot. The bluetick somersaulted backward, landing in a mess, oozing from its shattered skull. As the rest of the pack caught up to Gypsum and saw the dead hound with its brain sprayed across the ice, most of them reared back and cowered in the pines, whimpering like pups. Mayeaux picked them off. The last two, in a panic, wound up in a deep part of the creek, scrabbling at boulders too slick to purchase. After Mayeaux killed them, they turned slowly in the current, catching on a log. Back in the trees, one of the bitches was howling from a gut wound; Mayeaux sent a last bullet through her neck and then at last the woods were quiet. All around him, hot brass burrowed narrow tunnels in the snow.

HENRY PARSON LEANED back in his chair with his boots on the desk, phone in his lap. The receiver had one of those curvaceous shoulder-rest accessories that had always struck the sheriff as somehow sexual or feminine or both, but which he made use of anyway now, seeing as no one was around.

It was time to call. Almost a week had passed since Dave Campbell and Leo DeMint had shown up at the station. Henry had been tempted to inform Hannah Tucker that same day. If nothing else, it was an excuse to talk to her. The news, though, put him in an awkward spot. No way around it: it was embarrassing. The pig farmer's widow had been right about Tom Mayeaux all along—while he, Henry Parson, a twenty-year lawman and the elected county sheriff, had dismissed her suspicions out of hand. Henry cringed to recall the numerous occasions on which he had reassured Hannah in the condescending style of someone who'd seen it all before—telling her it was only natural, she was looking for a reason, somebody to blame.

Even after Dave had told him what he'd witnessed that day from up on the ridge, Henry'd been reluctant to believe it. (Neither Campbell nor DeMint was exactly a model citizen himself, and it was not beyond the possible that they were out to settle some unrelated beef with Tom.) But then, when the sheriff drove out to the Tucker place to have a chat with him, he'd found the Airstream empty, the flatbed missing, Mayeaux long gone.

That day in the sty, Mayeaux must have lied about where he was from. Henry had failed to locate any relatives. He'd tracked down his old commanding officer, a major now, who only had the vaguest recollection of Mayeaux. The major had given Henry a contact for Mayeaux's old platoon leader, and that man had gone on and on about Tom—couldn't say enough for him, exemplary soldier that he'd been.

Exemplary.

Henry dialed the number. How was he going to explain this to her? What manner should he affect—a friend's? In what tone of voice was Henry going to tell Hannah Tucker that there were indications the boy he was now convinced had killed her husband was also living in her house, sleeping in her bed, using her things? Should he mention the buck head in the fireplace, its hide singed black, the plastic nose and eyeballs melted?

No. He'd just urge her not to worry and swear that they would find him. No empty promise, that. Where, after all, could Tom Mayeaux go?

TOTAL SOLAR

WAS STARING AT A BROWN SKY. JUST MOMENTS EARLIER a researcher from the United Nations Ornithological Department had told me that fecal particulate from the city's open sewage system made up an alarming proportion of the atmosphere in Kabul. The researcher was the sort of person who would say, "If you really want something to write about . . ." or "You're looking for a story? What if I were to tell you . . ." as if, before meeting him, you had lived in darkness, scribbling claptrap of zero consequence to anybody. He'd invited me to lunch because he had some urgent information regarding birds. Something to do with the great migrations above the Hindu Kush, the desertification of Iranian wetlands, mass extinction. "Have you ever seen a Siberian crane?" he asked me. "No, you haven't. No one in Afghanistan has seen a Siberian crane in the past seventy years."

I pretended to take notes. My notepad, back then, was mostly pretend notes. Many of the pages featured detailed sketches of me killing myself by various means. One especially tedious interview—with a mullah, another fucking mullah holding forth behind a vertical index finger—had yielded a kind of comic strip of me leaping from a skyscraper, shooting myself midair, and landing in front of a bus.

A waiter appeared and asked whether we wanted any coffee. He wore an anachronistic tribal costume and a prayer cap adorned with sequins. The garb complemented the restaurant's verdant rose garden, the pleasantly burbling fountain, and the private gazebo in which we sat, the researcher and I, surrounded by paisley tapestries.

"I already told you I don't drink coffee," the researcher said. "I wanted pomegranate juice."

"One pomegranate juice?" the waiter asked.

"Not *now*. Now it's too late." The researcher pointed at his plate. "Now I've eaten."

"No pomegranate juice?" the waiter asked.

"No pomegranate juice," the researcher said. "Bring me a green tea. Can you manage a green tea?"

"One Afghan chai."

"I'll have one as well," I said.

"Two Afghan chai."

As soon as the waiter turned his back, the researcher rolled his eyes. "*Afghan chai.* It's Lipton, for Christ's sake. I'm sorry, what was I saying? Ah, yes, you've never seen a Siberian crane . . ."

I returned to my sketch. A few days ago, I'd posted a minor web item about a contractor who'd got himself decapitated while transporting a duffel bag full of cash across the Kandahari Desert. There was a new technique, seemed. Rather than a knife, they used wire. They looped the wire around your neck, stepped on your back, and pulled up with a rapid sawing motion. Picture a bowler polishing a bowling ball. Anyway, I was trying to draw the researcher doing this to me (while, at the same time, I double-fisted a bottle of rat poison and a bottle of arsenic), but I was distracted by the gardener, a bearded man dressed in the same traditional robes as the waiter, roaming the grounds with a pair of clippers. Every couple of steps, the gardener would pause, seat the stem of a rose between the two blades, begin to squeeze, think better, release the stem, and continue on his way. I watched him do this maybe half a dozen times.

My failure to sympathize with the birds—which, thanks to the drones and the Arabs and the fecal particulate, appeared to be suffering an unprecedented genocide—was no doubt attributable in part to my hangover. The night before, I'd stayed too long at the Norwegian embassy. I'd been trying to get into the pantsuit of a consultant for the World Bank. She was new to Kabul and, I sensed, typically stimulated by the proximity of violence and privation. (Not the reality, never the reality—the *proximity*.) Hours of careful effort had been undermined by a brief, emasculating incident at the snacks table. We were loading up our paper napkins when a drunk Frenchman stumbled over and began dipping pieces of bruschetta into the bowl of tomato salad. I knew this Frenchman. He was into gemstones or helicopter parts or some such, and he was a dangerous, erratic alcoholic. Therefore, although the Frenchman was polluting the tomato salad with his dirty French fingernails and even his hairy French knuckles, I pretended not to notice. Not so my consultant. The thing to do was use a fork, she communicated to the Frenchman by offering him one. The Frenchman smiled at us both, took the fork, and stabbed it in the wall, where it stuck like a dart. Then he sank his fist into the bowl of tomato salad, all the way to the wrist, and turned it like a pestle before lifting out a dripping handful. This the Frenchman brutally flung on the bruschetta, which, when he offered it to me, I somehow lacked the courage to decline.

"Coffee?" the waiter said. I looked up to see him placing two steaming mugs on our table. The researcher drew a breath.

———

I WAS STARING at a brown sky. I sat up. The first thing I noticed was a leg. It stood a yard from me, still socked and shoed, as if it had come detached midstride. Next I saw the hole in the wall. It looked as if a wrecking ball had been swung through. Cinder blocks and sandbags and concertina wire all lay in a dusty heap. A dog sat on top of the heap. The dog—one of those Kabuli street hounds glistening with bald patches, a tumor the size of a cantaloupe hanging between its haunches, and no doubt an ear infection that caused it to list and wander in psychotic circles— was barking mutely. I realized I was deaf. All I could detect was a high-pitched tone, like a test of the emergency broadcast system. The emergency broadcast system? I thought. Jesus, I was getting old. Then I wondered: *Tinnitus*—rhymes with "hit us" or "smite us"?

Maybe this was only a test.

I was watching a woman pull a long splinter out of her cheek. It kept coming out, like a magic trick.

"Sue?" I said.

It was Sue Kwan, from Human Rights Watch. She'd been at the Norwegian embassy. I'd bluntly propositioned her after abasing myself in front of the World Bank consultant. Kwan had rebuffed me so gently, with such pity. I'd responded by calling her latest report biased and confusingly structured.

Now she looked at me, wide-eyed, unable to answer on account of the splinter.

"I'm sorry, Sue," I said.

I can only imagine how absurd it must have sounded. Sue, though, seemed not to have heard me either. I followed her gaze back to the hole in the wall. Several men with rifles were climbing over the rubble, into the garden.

———

SUE KWAN WAS a good source. She always gave me early drafts of her reports, despite her organization's rules against doing so. Furthermore, her motives, unlike those of most of us, weren't really suspect. She was not stimulated by the proximity of violence and privation. A genuine person, Kwan: she was there to help. Of course, I often went around deriding her for being stupid and naïve.

I remember this one time, we were sharing a taxi, sitting in traffic after a party at the Dutch embassy, when a street urchin carrying a crate of eggs collapsed on the sidewalk and began convulsing and foaming at the mouth. The old fake-a-seizure gimmick—but Sue fell for it. She got out of the taxi and crouched over the boy.

"Sue, get back in the car!" I shouted.

"He needs help," she said.

"It's a trick," I told her. "It's fake."

And here Sue turned on me a look that I recognized immediately. It was the look I'd always imagined God would have were I ever forced to meet Him.

"So what?" she said.

So what!

Maybe she wasn't so stupid, naïve. But then, why had she raised her hand? Why was she waving at the men with guns climbing through the wall? Did she actually think they were there to help? Or could it be that Sue was offering herself, at last making the sacrifice she'd been put on earth to make?

"No, Sue," I said.

She paid no heed. She kept waving. One of the men lifted his rifle and shot her in the stomach. Sue slumped forward, and the man walked up and shot her in the head. That was the end of Sue Kwan. That was the death of one of the few genuine, unsuspect people I encountered during all my time over there.

Or one of the stupidest, the most naïve.

The gunmen were clean-shaven, clad in normal city attire. There were four of them. Each had a Kalashnikov with a banana clip duct-taped upside down to another banana clip. This way, when the first banana clip was empty, he could simply eject and flip it over, rather than having to fumble around in his pocket or what-have-you, wasting precious shooting time.

One wore an opalescent vest that seemed to shimmer and undulate in the sunlight. What was opalescent and seemed to shimmer and undulate in the sunlight? Pearls, I thought.

Then I thought: ball bearings.

They did not dally, these four. They got right down to killing. The gunman who'd shot Kwan appeared to be the leader. He yelled instructions to his comrades, who fanned out and started finishing off the survivors of the blast. I watched them execute a fat American who looked vaguely familiar. Yes, he was DEA, an adviser or analyst working on the poppy problem. He was down among the roses, bloody and weeping. When the gunman loomed over him, pointing the muzzle at his face, this fellow did the most peculiar thing. He grasped the travel wallet that hung around his neck—a transparent window on the front displaying his security-clearance badge—and held it up.

It was around this time that I lay back down in the grass. I don't know how long I lay there. My eyes were shut. There was the tone, was all there was—the tone and, somewhere beyond the tone, the faint pop of rifles like I was underwater, I was underground. Tinnitus or tinnitus? Smite us or hit us? Years before, I'd made the mistake of doing a live piece-to-camera for CNN. While reading the cue card I'd written for myself, I'd pronounced "misled" as if it rhymed with "guy's old." On the progress of the war in Afghanistan, the successes of the surge, the president had *myzled* the public. The YouTube video had been viewed many, many times—many more times, certainly, than any story I'd ever reported. That fucking YouTube video was going to be my legacy.

Imagine: the vanity, the *inanity*, of these final meditations. YouTube! Well, Sue Kwan wasn't the only one who would die as she had lived.

I felt a kind of thwump reverberate from the earth into my body, and a hot cushion of air lifted me off the ground. It lifted me and transported me somewhere else and set me down.

I sat up. I opened my eyes.

IT WAS DIFFICULT to see in all the dust and debris. It felt like nighttime. But not exactly nighttime—more like an eclipse, a total solar. Dark figures, silhouettes, flitted about. As the air began to clear I saw that they were pouring into the garden through the hole in the wall. Most of them wore uniforms— they were soldiers, police. The shooting seemed to have stopped. I got to my feet. I was a little wobbly, a little wobbly. I tried a couple of steps, then a couple more. I tripped on something and stumbled to the ground. When I looked back to see what it was, I discovered an arm. First the leg—now this, an arm. I knew there must be heads around. For once, I didn't want to see them; just knowing they were around was enough.

The arm looked as if it had been sprayed with buckshot. Silver was embedded in the flesh. I thought of pearls in a mollusk. (Not pearls, though, I thought.) A tactical-looking watch was still strapped around the wrist. I knew that watch. It belonged to the researcher from the United Nations Ornithological Department.

OK, stop looking at the arm.

I got up again. No one seemed to notice me. I scaled the

rubble pile. I walked right past the soldiers and police, through the hole in the wall, and into the street.

There were vehicles everywhere—mostly Toyota Hiluxes, but also up-armored Humvees with machine-gun turrets, Mine-Resistant Ambush Protected personnel carriers, and SUVs whose tinted windows were decorated with portraits of illustrious war criminals. Commanders screamed into their radios, subordinates rushed around, limp corpses were loaded into trucks. The first TV crews had already arrived—a few local teams and the BBC. They were prepping their gear, jostling for position. One of the screaming commanders spotted them, holstered his radio, brought a comb out of his breast pocket, and headed over, combing his hair.

I'd avoided the TV crowd ever since the whole CNN episode, and now I turned away, hoping they hadn't seen me. There was something else, too. I was, for some reason, embarrassed. Not misled/myzled embarrassed; more naked-in-a-dream embarrassed. The source of my naked-in-a-dream embarrassment was never the nakedness. It was the fact that I alone had managed to get myself into such a situation, while everyone else on the submarine or whatever had managed to avoid it. What did it say about me, the sort of person I was?

I had arrived at the end of the block. I stood there, unsure what to do next. Walk back to the TV crews and the commanders and the subordinates? Wander up from nowhere, tap one of them on the shoulder, and explain that I had been in the garden, I had survived the attack, I came from the other side of the wall? After a while, it struck me that my only option was to keep going.

———

IT WAS STARTING to get dark. I passed men fanning coals at street-side kebab stands, fruit vendors, toy stores, cobblers repairing sandals on the sidewalk outside of the mosque. I experienced the drug-and-urine fragrances of the park, and the fryer fragrance of the Chief Burger. Amid the gridlocked traffic, boys swung canisters of holy smoke and older men hawked wares. One of the wares was dolls. The dollmonger carried dozens of them, a towering bouquet of dolls, each blue-eyed and blond-haired, dressed in pink and affecting an erotically ruminative expression. I followed him until he vanished into the miasma of fecal particulate hanging in the headlights like fog.

Soon I reached the river, the bazaar. Here I felt as I often had: that I could move among the buyers and sellers, the teenagers perusing defunct American military gear, without attracting their attention. But then, you always felt you could, didn't you, until you discovered that no, actually, you never could? A friend of mine, a local reporter, was once hired by a visiting documentarian to fix and translate. This documentarian was enchanted by Afghanistan—within a week, enchanted. One day she told my friend that she wanted to film some B-roll at the bazaar. She needed happy, normal Afghans, she explained, living happy, normal lives. My friend was busy and could not accompany her. Against his emphatic advice, the documentarian went alone. She went, she filmed, she laughed with the vendors, she ate the mangoes, and she drank the juice. Then, when her memory sticks were full, her bag laden with textiles, she returned to her guesthouse, triumphant. "See?" she said to my friend.

It was not until about a month later, while my friend was transcribing her footage, that he came to the B-roll from that day and saw the man speaking into his cell phone. He appeared in almost every frame, following the documentarian from stall to stall. He held the cell phone to his ear, yelling over the din of the crowd. "Yes, she's here alone," the man yelled. "Yes, she's American," he yelled. "No, no one is with her, I can easily grab her, no problem. Fine, I'll wait. Call me back when they decide."

By the time I reached the outskirts of the bazaar, several children were tugging on my sleeve. Although I still couldn't hear, I knew what they were saying. They were saying, "One dollar!" and "Hey, fuck you!" I tried to shoo them. A boy in a soiled tracksuit flopped to the ground. His legs flailed; spit bubbled on his lips. I increased my pace, practically jogging into the lightless neighborhoods below the mountain.

THE LABYRINTH OF alleys sloped up the foothills, and the mud-mortar homes became denser, muddier, as the grade became steeper. I found myself at the bottom of an earthen staircase hacked into the cliffside. The stairs ascended precipitously, disappearing into more crowded dwellings. Several steps above me, a dog squatted. I knew that dog. It had the same glistening bald patches, same cantaloupe-size tumor hanging down between its haunches. Well, they all did. The tumor was so large that it bumped against the steps as the dog limped painfully up them.

I followed. In places, the stairs more nearly resembled a ladder. The boulders and crags through which they carved were marked with paint by the de-miners. But "clear" or "not clear"? The marks were illegible—to me, in any case. Homes of IDPs stood improbably amid the sheer escarpments, and their sullage trickled down the stairs, making them slippery. At some point the air changed. I felt the difference in my lungs, which welcomed rather than cringed from each inhalation. I looked back. The dim city lay far below. So did the pollution, the particulate.

I was gazing down on that foul soup, putrefying in the basin of the Hindu Kush.

I suppose that that must have been when I saw them, the birds. They banked in unison, right at eye-level, perfectly synchronized, showing the white undersides of their wings, the dark tops. They swooped down the mountain, over the hovels, the city, the bazaar. Then they came soaring back, riding an updraft with an exquisite minimum of effort. As the flock passed overhead I realized that my hearing had returned. I detected what I thought were bells—yes, bells: a tinny music that seemed to harmonize with the flight of the birds.

I don't know how long I watched and listened to them. It was a while, anyway, before I spotted the elderly man standing on the roof, conducting them. There's no other word for it: he was conducting those birds. He even had a batonlike instrument—a horsewhip or something—with tassels hanging from its tip. He flourished the instrument, and to each movement the birds responded, banking toward him, or away. When, in a crisp, martial motion, he brought the tassels down against his thigh, the flock collapsed upon the roof, as if sucked into a drain.

THE MAN'S HOUSE stood across the moonscape mountainside. I scrabbled over the painted boulders and the loose, eroding shale. When I arrived, I found that the house, too, was constructed of boulders and loose, eroding shale. I knocked on the door. It opened. The man held a bird in each fist. They were pigeons, I saw, and attached with wire to their ankles were miniature silver bells.

The man possessed magnificent eyebrows, which projected straight out of his face and then curved upward, like saplings that sprout from a bluff and yearn for the sun. He spoke to me.

My hearing was almost entirely restored—but of course, like the documentarian, I was deaf. I always had been.

The old man seemed to get that I was in some sort of trouble. He stepped back into his house and gestured with one of the pigeons for me to enter. I removed my shoes and followed him into a small room paved with cushions. The sole illumination came from a vase of flowers plugged into an electrical outlet. The flowers were a lamp. At the end of each artificial stem, translucent petals enveloped a magenta light. The man opened his hands and the pigeons fluttered loose, beating their wings across the small, magenta room and out the door, returning to their coop.

The man was staring at my chest. I looked and saw that my shirt had blood on it. Quite a lot of blood. The man's eyebrows professed concern.

"There was an attack," I said. I pointed down the mountain. "Down there." I pressed my hands together, as if in prayer, and pulled them apart in a reverse clap. "Boom," I said.

"Boom?" the man said.

"Boom," I said.

Finally, we understood each other.

THE OLD MAN invited me to lie down on one of the cushions, and as soon as I did fatigue overtook me. I don't know how long I was out. It felt like seconds; it might have been centuries. Anway, enough time passed for everything to have changed. When I woke, I saw right away that I never should have gone to sleep; I'd made a terrible mistake in trusting the old man.

The agents stood over me, whispering to one another. Two of them had on the black paramilitary uniforms and combat boots of the National Directorate of Security, and between them towered a third man, in slacks, a blue blazer, and a white Oxford shirt. Under the blazer, he wore a leather shoulder holster with the handgrip of a pistol sticking out.

When they saw that I was awake they stopped talking. The two uniformed agents bent down, each grabbing me under an arm, and roughly hauled me to my feet. The plainclothes agent regarded me.

"Passport," he said.

I reached into the pocket where I normally kept it. I smiled apologetically. "I'm very sorry," I said, "I seem to have—"

"No passport?" the agent said.

He took a deep breath through his nose, such a breath that he seemed to increase in height by several inches. Then he grabbed a handful of my shirt, violently twisted it around his fist, and held it up before my eyes, showing me the blood. He shouted furiously into my face words I couldn't understand but whose meaning I could guess.

I started to explain. Before I got very far, the agent reared back and with the hand that was not wrapped in my shirt slapped me so hard that I could taste his palm, a mix of sweat and Purell, in the back of my throat.

"If you'll allow me to—"

Again he slapped me. This time the tone returned, accompanied by lights. I slackened my jaw, trying to pop my ears. When my vision cleared I glimpsed, for the first time, the old man standing behind the agents. I looked at him imploringly, silently entreating him to intervene. To my horror, however, I discovered that the eyebrows did not in fact profess concern, that they had never professed concern, that that had just been a kind of wishful thinking on my part.

———

It turned out there was a road behind the house. A Hilux was parked on it. The two uniformed agents handcuffed me and stuffed me in the back. We headed down the mountain. The uniformed agents rode in the bed while the plainclothes agent drove. In the city, there were a lot of checkpoints, more than usual. Each time we approached one, a policeman would peer into the Hilux, recognize the plainclothes agent, stiffen, and wave us through.

We turned onto a narrow lane hemmed in on both sides by sandbags and blast wall. Toward the end of the lane, we had to zig and zag to maneuver past staggered barriers. At a gate a policeman peered into the cab of the Hilux, recognized the plainclothes agent, stiffened, and waved us through.

I was guided by the uniformed agents into a bleak, institutional tower, down a hall, down a flight of stairs, down another hall, and into a poorly lit room. The door slammed and a bolt clacked into place. The room was square, concrete, furnished with a metal table and two metal chairs. I knew this room. No, I'd never actually been inside it—I had never dreamed that I would!—but I knew it.

"I'm an American," I heard myself say. The words echoed: *I'm an American, I'm an American.* Later, in a feebler voice, trying to avoid the echo, I heard myself add, "I'm a journalist."

The door opened and the plainclothes agent strode in. He carried a bulky accordion folder under his arm. He set the folder on the table, undid the elastic band, and reached inside. He extracted a Ziploc bag pinched between his thumb and forefinger, opened it, and extracted a US passport. He slid the passport across the table, inviting me, I gathered, to have a look.

It was mine, of course. They must have found it at the restaurant. I began to explain. The agent walked around the table and slapped me in the face.

———

THE NEXT THING he pulled out of the accordion folder and slid across the table was a document, too thick for staples, in Dari or Pashto, I had no idea which. Then he pulled out a fountain pen, unscrewed the top, and slid that over, too.

I flipped to the last page of the document and signed it. The agent wasn't satisfied. He leaned forward and tapped the bottom right corner of the top page. Then he turned to the second page and did the same. I understood that he wished me to initial each one. It took a long time. First I had trouble getting the hang of the fountain pen; then, midway through, my hand began to cramp. I had to set the pen down and try to shake out the cramp, which was awkward with the handcuffs. The agent grew impatient. When he stood up and walked over to my side of the table, I flinched and cowered, anticipating the blow. Instead of slapping me, however, the agent took my hand in both of his and gently but firmly massaged my palm with his callused thumbs. That helped a lot, and soon I was initialing again.

How I wish I could say that it felt good to confess! I'd taken so much from these people, their country, this war. I'd taken and taken. Still, it didn't feel good. It felt false.

Once I'd initialed all the pages, the agent picked up the stack, shuffled it into line, and returned it to the folder. He left the room without a word, and his two colleagues entered. They escorted me down the hall, up the flight of stairs, down the other hall, and out of the building. One of them removed my handcuffs and gave me my passport. The other pointed at the gate.

I WAS SO exhausted and demoralized that I paid little attention to where I was going. I stumbled through the park, past the

Chief Burger and the toy stores. At one point, I crossed paths with a pack of orphans. I must not have looked too hot: they regarded me dubiously, uncertain whether to beg.

When I reached the mosque, one of the cobblers sitting on the sidewalk pointed at my feet. I'd been barefoot ever since the agents had whisked me away from the pigeon conductor. With the cobbler pointing and laughing and his fellow cobblers starting to join in and pedestrians stopping to see and cars slowing down and mullahs and would-be mullahs frowning at me from the ablution area, I was visited by a familiar embarrassment.

The cobbler held up a pair of sandals, offering them to me. I pulled my pockets inside-out to show him they were empty. He waved the sandals, insisting that I take them. I was choked with gratitude; I nearly wept. I struggled to summon the words while the cobbler waited to receive them.

That's when I saw the man talking on his cell phone.

"No, no one is with him, I can easily grab him," the man was saying.

Or was he? I didn't know. I still don't.

Acknowledgments

MANY GRATEFUL THANKS TO MY FRIENDS IN Afghanistan who so patiently unburdened me of so much ignorance (and who still live in a country that is too perilous for me to be able to name them here).

And to those who helped these stories along the way: Joel Lovell, Tim Duggan, Andrew Wylie, James Verini, Boris Fishman, Emily Stokes, Chad Benson, Willing Davidson, Ezra Carlsen, and Lorin Stein.

And to my family, whom I don't deserve: Stan, Lucia, Jake, Andrew, Tom, Therese, and Nama.

Permissions

About the Author

Luke Mogelson is a contributing writer at *The New York Times Magazine* and was a recipient of the National Magazine Award in 2014. His fiction has appeared in *The New Yorker, The Paris Review, The Hudson Review, The Missouri Review*, and *The Kenyon Review*. Mogelson served as a medic in the 69th Infantry, New York Army National Guard, from 2007 to 2010.